D0845177

come on in!

Septuagenarian Stew: Stories & Poems *(1990)*

The Last Night of the Earth Poems *(1992)*

Screams from the Balcony: Selected Letters, 1960–1970 *(1993)*

Pulp *(1994)*

Living on Luck: Selected Letters, 1960s–1970s (Volume 2) *(1995)*

Betting on the Muse: Poems & Stories *(1996)*

Bone Palace Ballet: New Poems *(1997)*

The Captain Is Out to Lunch and the Sailors Have Taken Over
the Ship *(1998)*

Reach for the Sun: Selected Letters, 1978–1994 (Volume 3) *(1999)*

What Matters Most Is How Well You Walk Through the Fire:
New Poems *(1999)*

Open All Night: New Poems *(2000)*

Night Torn Mad with Footsteps: New Poems *(2001)*

Beerspit Night and Cursing: The Correspondence of Charles Bukowski
and Sheri Martinelli, 1960–1967 *(2001)*

sifting through the madness for the word, the line, the way:
new poems *(2003)*

The Flash of Lightning Behind the Mountain *(2004)*

Slouching Toward Nirvana *(2005)*

come on in!

charles bukowski

new poems

edited by john martin

HarperCollins books may be purchased for educational, business, or sales promotional use. For information, please write: Special Markets Department, HarperCollins Publishers, 10 East 53rd Street, New York, NY 10022.

FIRST EDITION

Designed by Cassandra J. Pappas

Printed on acid-free paper

Library of Congress Cataloging-in-Publication Data
Bukowski, Charles.
    Come on in!: new poems / Charles Bukowski.—1st ed.
      p.cm.
    ISBN-10: 0-06-057705-3
    ISBN-13: 978-0-06-057705-6
    I. Title.
    PS3552.U4C57 2006
    811'.54—dc22   2005051110

06 07 08 09 10 ❖/RRD 10 9 8 7 6 5 4 3 2 1

These poems are part of an archive of unpublished work that Charles Bukowski left to be published after his death.

Grateful acknowledgment is made to John Martin, who edited these poems.

contents

**I live near the
slaughterhouse
and am ill
with thriving.**

she looked at me and asked,
did you?
did you?
did you?

**it's a lonely world
of frightened people.**

**I will never have
a house in the valley
with little stone men
on the lawn.**

come on in!

I live near the

slaughterhouse

and am ill

with thriving.

come on in!

welcome to my wormy hell.
the music grinds off-key.
fish eyes watch from the wall.
this is where the last happy shot was
fired.
the mind snaps closed
like a mind snapping
closed.
we need to discover a new will and a new
way.
we're stuck here now
listening to the laughter of the
gods.
my temples ache with the fact of
the facts.
I get up, move about, scratch
myself.
I'm a pawn.
I am a hungry prayer.
my wormy hell welcomes you.
hello. hello there. come in, come on in!
plenty of room here for us all,
sucker.
we can only blame ourselves so
come sit with me in the dark.
it's half-past
nowhere
everywhere.

nothing but a scarf

long ago, oh so long ago, when
I was trying to write short stories
and there was one little magazine which printed
decent stuff
and the lady editor there usually sent me
encouraging rejection slips
so I made a point to
read her monthly magazine in the public
library.

I noticed that she began to feature
the same writer
for the lead story each
month and
it pissed me off because I thought that I could
write better than that
fellow.
his work was facile and bright but it had no
edge.
you could tell that he had never had his nose rubbed into
life, he had just
glided over it.

next thing I knew, this ice-skater-of-a-writer was
famous.

he had begun as a copy boy
on one of the big New York
magazines

(how the hell do you *get* one of those
jobs?)

then he began appearing in some of the best
ladies' magazines
and in some of the respected literary
journals.

then after a couple of early books
out came a little volume, a sweet
novelette, and he was truly
famous.

it was a tale about high society and
a young girl and it was
delightful and charming and just a bit
naughty.

Hollywood quickly made a movie out of
it.

then the writer bounced around Hollywood
from party to party
for a few years.
I saw his photo again and again:
a little elf-man with huge
eyeglasses.
and he always wore a long dramatic
scarf.

but soon he went back to New York and to all the
parties there.

he went to every important party thereafter for years
and to
some that weren't very
important.

then he stopped writing altogether and just went
to parties.

he drank or doped himself into oblivion almost
every night.

his once slim frame more than doubled in
size.
his face grew heavy and he no longer looked
like the young boy with the quick and dirty
wit but more like an
old frog.

the scarf was still on display but his hats were
too large and came down almost to his
eyes;
all you noticed was his
twisted
lurid
grin.

the society ladies still liked to drag him
around New York
one on each arm
and
drinking like he did, he didn't live
to enjoy his old age.

so
he died
and was quickly
forgotten

until somebody found what they claimed was his secret
diary / novel

and then all the famous people in
New York were very
worried

and they should have been worried because when it
was published
out came all the dirty
laundry.

but I still maintain that he never really did know *how* to
write; just what and
when and about
whom.

slim, thin
stuff.

ever so long ago, after reading
one of his short stories,
after dropping the magazine to the floor,
I thought,
Jesus Christ, if this is what they
want,
from now on
I might as well write for
the rats and the spiders
and the air and just for
myself.

which, of course, is exactly what
I did.

literary chitchat

my friend Tom, he liked to come over
and he'd say, "let's go get a coffee."
and my girlfriend would say, "you guys
going to talk that literary stuff again?"
and we'd go to this place where you paid
for your first coffee and all the refills were
free
and we'd get a seat by the window and he
would begin:
Hemingway, Faulkner, Fitzgerald, Dos
Passos mainly but others got in there
too: e. e. cummings, Ezra Pound, Dreiser,
Jeffers, Céline and so forth.
although I will admit I was mostly a
listener and wondered what he was
really getting at, if anything, I
continued to listen and
drink coffee after
coffee.
once he said, "look, I'll take you to the
place Fitzgerald stayed at for a while
during his Hollywood period."
"all right," I said and we got into his
car and he drove me there and pointed
it out:
"Fitzgerald lived there."
"all right," I said and then he drove us
back for more coffee.
Tom was truly excited about these
literary figures of the past.
I was too, to an extent,
but as Tom talked on and on about
them

and the coffees continued unabated
my interest began to wane, more than
wane.
I began to want to get rid of
Tom.

it was easy.
one day I wrote a poem about Tom
and it was published and he read
it
and after that
we enjoyed no more coffees
together.

Tom had been working on a
biography of me
and that ended that.
then another writer came along
and he drank my wine
and didn't talk about Hemingway,
Fitzgerald, Faulkner, etc.,
he talked about himself
and ended up writing a not-very-
satisfactory biography
of me.

I should have stuck with Tom.

no, I should have gotten rid of
both of them.

which is exactly what I have
done.

this machine is a fountain

my system is always the same:
keep it loose
write a great number of
poems
try with all your
heart and
don't worry about the
bad
ones.

keep it going
keep it
hot
forget about immortality
if you ever
remembered
it.

the sound of this machine is
good.

much paper
more desire.

just
hammer away and wait for lady
luck.

what a
bargain.

200 years

hunched over this white sheet of paper
at 4 in the afternoon. I
received a letter from a young poet this morning
informing me that I was one of the most
important writers of the last
200 years.
well, now, one can't believe that
especially if one has felt as I have
this past month,
walking about,
thinking,
surely I am going crazy,
and then thinking,
I can't write
anymore.

and then I remember the factories,
the production lines,
the warehouses,
the time clocks,
overtime and layoffs
and flirtations with the Mexican girls
on the assembly line;
each day everything was carefully planned,
there was always something to do,
there was more than enough to do,
and if you didn't keep up,
if you weren't clever and swift and
obedient
you were out with the sparrows and
the bums.

writing's different, you're floating out there in the
white air, you're hanging from the high-wire,
you're sitting up in a tree and they're working at
the trunk with a power
saw . . .

there's no silk scarf about one's neck,
no English accent,
no remittance checks from aristocratic ladies in Europe
with blind and impotent
husbands.

it's more like a fast hockey game
or putting on the gloves with a man
50 pounds heavier and ten years
younger, or
it's like steering a ship through the fog
with a mad damsel clinging to your
neck

and all along you know you've gotten away
with some quite obvious stuff, that
you've been given undeserved credit, for stuff
that you either wrote offhand or
hardly meant or hardly cared
about.

well, it helps to be
lucky.

yet, on the other hand, you have sometimes
done it as you always knew it should
be done, and you knew then that it was
as good as it could be done,
and that maybe you *had* done it better,
in a way,
than anybody else had done it for a long time
and
you allowed yourself to feel
good about that
for a moment or
two.

they put the pressure on you
with statements about 200 years,
and when only one individual says it, that's all
right
but when 2 or 3 or 4 say it—
that's when they tend to open the door to a
kookoo bin.
they tell you to give up cigarettes and
booze, and then they tell you that you
have 25 more good years ahead of you and
then
perhaps ten more years to enjoy your old
age
as you suck on
the rewards and
memories.

Patchen's gone, we need you, man,
we all need you for that

good feeling just above the
belly button—
knowing that you are there in some small room in
northern California writing poems and
killing flies with a torn
flyswatter.

they can kill you,
the praisers can kill you,
the young girls can kill you,
as the blue-eyed boys in English depts.
who send warm letters
handwritten
on lined paper
can kill you,
and they're all correct:
2 packs a day and the bottle
can kill you
too.

of course,
anything can kill you
and something eventually
will. all I can say is that
today
I have just inserted a new
typewriter ribbon
into this old machine
and I am pleased with the way it
works and that makes for more than just an
ordinary day, thank
you.

residue

there's an old movie
based on a Hemingway short story
I saw the beginning of it
again on late night /
early morning tv
but the fellow who plays
Hem
his ears aren't right
neither are
his chin
his hair
his voice;
and there's this lovely
wench
in the film
with perfect buns
whose role it is to
endure his precious
literary abuse
while he slowly dies in the
African jungle.

I click the movie off.

of course, I never met
Hemingway.
maybe he was like that fellow.
I hope
not.

then I look about my bedroom and
think, Jesus Jesus,
why am I so upset by this
lousy tv movie?

what did I want them to make him
look like?
act like?
he was just a journalist from
Michigan who liked to shoot
big game
and his last kill was his
biggest;
surely he would have deserved the
nice buns
and the adoring eyes
of that actress who
he never saw and
who
in real life
later
drank herself to
death.

(the actor
who plays Hem
in the film is
still around
however
but barely
functioning.)

I guess when I look at that
movie
all I can think of to say
is:

bwana, bring me a
drink.

Coronado Street: 1954

listen, I been in the navy and I never heard cussing like you and
your girlfriend, man, and it lasts all night, every night.
we got religious people here, children, decent working folk, you're
keeping them awake every night and look at this place! everything's
broken, when I evict you you've got to pay to replace everything, buddy!
what do you mean, you don't have no fucking money?
what do you buy all that booze with?
credit?
don't give me that!
listen, I want it so quiet in here tonight we'll be able to hear the
church mice pray!
what's that?
well, up yours too, buddy!
and you wanna know what?
I saw your old lady sucking some guy's banana in the alley!
you don't give a damn?
what do you give a damn about?
nothing?
what kind of shit is that, *nothing*!
did you get a lobotomy somewhere along the way?
I got a good mind to wipe up the floor with you!
you say I'm the one with a lobotomy?
hey, don't go closing the door on me, pal!
I own this fucking place!
OPEN UP, BUDDY! I'M COMING IN!
WHAT THE FUCK ARE YOU LAUGHING AT?
HEY, WHAT THE FUCK ARE YOU LAUGHING AT?

a vision

we are in the clubhouse
3rd race, 83 degrees in June,
they have just sent in a 40-to-1 shot
in a maiden race,
the tote has clicked 3 or 4 times,
the old general feeling of futility
has arrived early
and then a girl walks by
to the window to make a bet
her skirt is slit
almost to the waist
and as she walks
this
most beautiful leg
is exposed
it sneaks out as she walks
flashes and vanishes.
every male in the clubhouse
watches that leg.
the girl is with a woman
who looks like her mother
and her mother keeps close
to the side of the skirt
that is slit,
trying to block our view.

the girl makes her bet
turns and now the leg is on
the other side
along with her mother.

the girl disappears down an
aisle to her seat
as all around us
there is a rising,
silent applause.

then the applause stops
and like forsaken children
we go back to our
Racing Forms.

cut-rate drugstore: 4:30 p.m.

this woman at the counter ahead of me
was buying four pairs of panties:
yellow, pink, blue and orange.
the lady at the register kept picking up
the panties and
counting them:
one, two, three, four.
then she counted them again:
one, two, three, four.
will there be anything else?
she asked the lady who was buying the
panties.
no, that's it, she answered.
no cigarettes or anything?
no, that's it.

the woman at the register
rang up the sale
collected the money
gave change
looked off into the distance
for a bit
and then she bent under the counter
and got a bag
and put the panties in this bag
one at a time—
first the blue pair, then the yellow,
then the orange, then the pink.

she looked at me next:
how are you doing today?
fair, I said.

is there anything else?
cigarettes?

all I want is what you see in front of
you.

I had hemorrhoid ointment
laxatives
and a box of paper clips.

she rang it up, took my money, made
change, bagged my things, handed them
to me.

have a nice day, she did not say.

and you too,
I said.

you can't tell a turkey by its feathers

son, my father said, if you only had some
ambition! you have no
get up and go! no
drive!
it's hard for me to believe that you are really
my son.

yeah, I
said.

I mean, he went on, how are you going to
make it?
your mother is worried sick and the neighbors
think you're some kind of
imbecile.
what are you going to
do?
we can't take care of you *all* your
life!

I'm 15 now, I told him, I won't be around
much longer.

but *look* at you, you just sit around in your room
all day! other
boys have jobs, paper routes, Jim Stover works
as an usher at the
Bayou!
HOW IN THE HELL ARE YOU GOING TO
SURVIVE IN THIS
WORLD?

I don't
know . . .

you make me SICK! sometimes, having a son like
you, I wish I was
dead.

well, he did die, he died more than 30 years
ago.

and last year I paid
$59,000 income
tax.

too early!

there are some people who will
phone a man at 7 a.m.
when he is desperately sick and
hungover.

I always greet
these idiots
with a few violent
words
and the slamming
down of the
receiver

knowing that their
morning eagerness
means that
they retired early
and thus wasted the
preceding
night

(and most likely
the preceding days, weeks and
years).

that they could
imagine
that
I'd want to
converse with

them
at 7 a.m.
is an insult
to
whatever
intelligent life
is left
in our dwindling
universe.

the green Cadillac

he hung the green Cadillac
almost straight up and down
standing on its nose
against the phone pole
next to the
All-American Hamburger
Hut.

I was
in the laundromat
with my girlfriend when
we heard the sound of it.

when we got there
the driver had
dropped out of the car
and run off.

and there was the
green Caddy
standing straight
up and down
against
the phone pole.

it was one of the most
magnificent sights
I had seen
in years:

in the 9 p.m. moonlight
it just stood there—

the people gathered
the people stood back
knowing the Caddy
could come crashing down
at any moment

but it didn't
it just stood there
straight as an arrow
alongside
the phone pole.

how the hell
they were going to get
that down
without wrecking it
was beyond me.

my girlfriend wanted to
wait and see how
they did it

but we hadn't
had dinner
yet
and I
talked her into
going back into the
laundromat and then
back to my place.

I was not
mechanically inclined
and it pissed
me off
to watch people
who were.

anyhow
about noon
the next day
when I went out to
buy a newspaper
the green Caddy
was gone.

there was just
an old bum
at the counter
in the All-American
having a coffee

but I had already seen
the real miracle
and I
walked back to
my place
satisfied.

I'm not all-knowing but . . .

one of the problems is
that when most people
sit down to write a poem
they think,
"now I am going to write a
poem"
and then
they go on to write a poem
that
sounds like a poem
or what they think
a poem should sound like.

this is one of their
problems.
of course, there are other
problems:
those writers of poems
that sound like poems
think that they then must
go around
reading them
to other people.

this, they say, is done
for status and recognition
(they are careful
not to mention
vanity
or the need for
instantaneous

approbation
from some
sparse, addled
crowd).

the best poems
it seems to me
are written out of
an ultimate
need.
and once the poem is
written,
the only need
after that
is to write
another.

and the silence
of the printed page
is the
best response
to a finished
work.

in decades past
I once warned
some poet-friends
of mine
about the masturbatory
nature of poetry readings
done just
for the applause of

a handful of
idiots.

"isolate yourself and
do your work and if you
must mix, then do it
with those who
have no interest at all
in what you consider
so
important."

such anger,
such a self-righteous
response
did I receive then
from my poet-friends
that it seemed to me
that I had exactly
proved my
point.

after that,
we all drifted
apart.

and that solved just
one of my
problems
and I suppose
just one of
theirs.

in the clubhouse

he is behind me,
talking to somebody:
"well, I like the 5 horse, he closed well last
time, I like a horse who can close.
but you know, you gotta kinda consider
the 4 and the 12.
the 4 needed his last race and look at
him, he's reading 40-to-1 now.
the 12's got a chance too.
and look at the 9, he looks really good,
really got a shine to his skin.
then too, you also gotta consider the 7 . . ."

every now and then I consider murdering
somebody, it just flashes in my mind for a
moment, then I dismiss it and rightfully
so.
I considered murdering the man who
belonged to the voice I heard,
then I worked on dismissing the thought.
and to make sure, I changed my seat,
I moved far down to my left,
I found a seat between a woman wearing a
sun shade and a young man violently
chewing on a mouthful of
gum.
then I felt
better.

a famished orphan sits somewhere in the mind

a heavyweight fighter called Young Stribling
was killed in the ring
so long ago
that I am certain
that I am the only one remembering him
tonight.

I am thinking of nobody else.

I sit here in this room and stare at the
lamp
and I think,
Stribling, Stribling.

outside
the starved palms continue to
decay
while in here
I remember and
watch a cigarette lighter,
an empty glass and a
wristwatch propped delicately on its
side.

Stribling.

son-of-a-bitch,
what causes me to think
about things like this?

I really don't need to know,
yet I wonder.

form letter

dear sir:
thank you for your manuscript
but this is to inform you
that I have no special influence
with any editor or publisher
and if I did
I would never dream of telling
them who or what
to publish.

I myself have never mailed any
of my work to anybody but
an editor or a publisher.
despite the fact that
my own work
was rejected for
decades,
I still never considered
mailing my work to
another writer
hoping that this other
writer might help me
get published.

and although I have
read some of what you
have mailed me
I return the work without
comment
except to ask

how did you get my
address?
and the effrontery
to mail me such
obvious
crap?

if you think me unkind,
fine.
and thank you for telling
me that I am a
great writer.

now you will have a
chance to re-evaluate
that opinion
and to choose another
victim.

first family

it's unholy.
I appear to be
lost. I walk from room to room and
there aren't many (2 or 3)
and she is in the dark room
snoring, I can't see her but her
mouth is open and her hair is gray
poor thing
and she doesn't mean me harm
least of all
does she mean me
harm,
and in the other room are
pink lips pink ears
on a head like a cabbage
and a child's blocks on the floor like
leprosy
and she also doesn't mean me any harm at
all,
but I cannot sleep and I sit in the kitchen
with a big black fly
that goes around and around and around
like a piece of snot grown a
heart,
and I am puzzled and not given to
cruelty (I'd like to think)
and I sit with the fly
under this yellow light
and we smoke a cigar and drink beer
and share the calendar with a frightened cat:
"katzen-unsere hausfrende: 1965."

I am a poor father because I want to stay alive as a
man but perhaps I never was a
man.

I suck on the cigar and suddenly the fly is gone
and there are just
the 3 of us
here.

a real thing, a good woman

I put the book down and ask:
why are they always writing about
the bulls, the bullfighters?
those who have never seen
them?
and as I break the web of the
spider reaching for my wine,
the hum of bombers
breaking the solace, I decide
I must write an impatient letter to my
priest about some 3rd St.
whore
who keeps calling me up at 3 in
the morning.
ass full of
splinters,
thinking of pocketbook poets
and the priest,
I go over to the typewriter
next to the window
to see to my letter
and look look
the sky's black as ink
and my wife says Brock, for
Christ's sake,
the typewriter all night,
how can I sleep? and I crawl quickly
into bed and
kiss her hair and say
sorry sorry sorry
sometimes I get excited

I don't know why . . .
a friend of mine has
written a book about
Manolete . . .
who's that? nobody, kid,
somebody dead
like Chopin or our old mailman
or a dog,
go to sleep, go to sleep,
and I kiss her and rub her
head,
a good woman,
and soon she sleeps as I wait
for morning.

a child's bedtime story

unsaid, said the snail.
untold, said the tortoise.
doesn't matter, said the tiger.
obey me, said the father.
be loyal, said the country.
watch me climb, said the vine.
doesn't matter, said the tiger.
untold, said the tortoise,
unsaid, said the snail.
I'll run, said the mouse.
I'll hide, said the cat.
I'll fly, said the sparrow.
I'll swim, said the whale.
obey and be loyal, said the
father and
everybody shut up! roared the
Queen.

the night came and all
the lights went out
as the cities
burned.

now, go to
sleep.

working out in Hades

holy Christ, I was on fire then and
I'd tell that whore I lived with on Beacon Street
starving and drinking
I'd tell her that I had something great and mysterious
going for me,
in fact, when I got really drunk I'd pace the floor in my
dirty torn shorts and ripped undershirt and
say more in desperation than belief: "I'm a fucking
genius and nobody knows it but
me!"

I thought this was rather humorous but she'd say, "honey, you're
full of shit, pour us another drink!"
she was crazy too and now and then an empty bottle would come
flying toward my head.
(she
missed most of the time)
but
when she bounced one off my skull I'd ignore it, and pour another
drink because
after all, when you're immortal, nothing
matters.
and besides, she had one of the finest pair of legs I'd ever
seen
in those high-heeled shoes and with her slender
ankles and her great knees glimmering in the
smoky drunken light.

she helped me through some of the worst times and if she was
here now we'd both laugh our goddamned asses
off
knowing it was all so true and real, and yet that somehow it
wasn't real at
all.

half-a-goldfish

we were out on the town
and we
went to this nice
house, lovely couple, etc.
anyhow, there were 7 or
8 of us and a jug of really
cheap wine
came out and then some
snacks, and then the man
got up and came back with
3 live goldfish and he said,
"watch this!"
and he put them in a large
fish tank
and the next thing I knew
there were 6 or 7 heads
down there glued to the fish tank
including my girlfriend's
and the soft light from the tank
shone on all the faces
and in all the eyes,
and one of the men went,
"ah!" and one of the girls
went, "oooh!"
some terrible thing was eating the
goldfish.
then somebody said, "look,
there's just half-a-goldfish
left and he's still swimming
around!"
I said, "why don't you fucking
party animals

get up off that rug
and help me finish this
cheap wine?"
12 or 14 eyes turned and looked at
me. then one at a time
the people moved away from
the fish tank and came back and sat
down at the table
again.

then they began a discussion about
the merits of
little literary
magazines.

lousy mail

the time comes when the tank runs
dry and you have to
refill
if you can.

the vulture swoops low over
you
as you open the manila envelope
from the ivy league university and
read:
"we have to pass on this batch of poems
but we are reading again in the
Fall."

"you were rejected?" asks my
wife.

"yes."

"well, fuck them," she says.

now, there's loyalty!

the vulture pauses in mid-flight,
defecates,
and flies out of the dining room
window.

and I think, it's nice that they'll be
reading again in the
Fall.

from the Dept. of English

we are surprised:
you used to jab with the left
then throw a left hook to the body
followed by an
overhand right.
we liked that
but we like your new way too:
where you can't tell where
the next punch
is coming
from.
to change your style like that when you're
not exactly a kid
anymore,
I think that takes some
doing.
anyhow, enough chitchat.
we're accepting your poems
for our departmental Literary Journal
and, by the way,
you are one of the poets selected for
class discussion
in our Contemporary Poetry Series.

no shit, baby?
well, suck my
titties.

and poems have too

don't worry, Dostoevsky,
the fish and the hills and the harbor
and the girls and the horses and the
alleys and the nights and the dogs
and the knives and the poisons and
the wines and the midgets and the
gamblers and the lights and the guns
and the lies and the sacrifices
and the flies and the frogs and the
flags and the doors and the windows
and the stairways and the cigarettes
and the hotels and myself have been
around a long time.

just like you.

poets to the rescue

the night the poets dropped by to say
hello
was at the time
that terrible time when
the ladies on the telephone
were screaming their fury
at me.

the night the poets came by to say
hello
I offered them cigarettes
as they talked about the
poet
who traveled all the way to Paris
in order to be able
to select the contents
of his next book
and we smiled at that
the poets and I
as we remembered starvation
dark mornings
deadly noons
evenings of elephantine
misery.

the night the poets came by to say
hello
we also mused about whatever happened to
Barney Google with the googly
eyes: he probably died for the love of
a strumpet as many good men
have

or went to London and walked in the
fog
waiting for
what?

the night the poets came by to say
hello
the walls were stained mellow with
grief
and beakers of curdled wine
dusty with dead spiders
sat about like memories best
forgotten.

the poets insisted then that it was best
not to think too much about things
or remember too much
but best just to sit around
in the evenings
and smoke our cigarettes and
drink our
beer
and talk quietly about
simple
things.

the poets
left soon after that
but the phone kept ringing
and I stood there frozen

as the ladies screamed their fury
at me.

what they wanted I didn't have
and what I had
they didn't want.

red hot mail

I continue to receive many letters
from young ladies.
evidently they have read some of
my books
but
they hardly ever
mention this.

many of their letters are
on pink or red
stationery
and they inform me that
they want to
kiss my lips and
they want to
come and stay with me
and
they say they will do anything
and everything
for and to me for
as long as
I can keep up with
them.
also, the younger ones are quick
to mention their
age: 21, 22, 23.

these letters are
fascinating, of
course,
but I always trash
them

for I know that all things
have their price
especially when they
are advertised as being
free.

besides,
what does it all mean?
bugs fuck, birds
fuck, horses
fuck, maybe some day they'll
find that
even wind, water and
rocks
fuck.

and
where were all these eager
girls
when I was starving,
broke, young and
alone?
they were
not born yet, of
course.
I can't blame them now
for
that.

but I do blame the girls
of my youth
for ignoring me and

for bedding down with all the
other
milkfish souls.
those other lads, I suppose,
were grateful then to
sink their spike into
any willing thing that
moved.

I only wish now some lass had
chanced upon me then
when I so needed her hair blowing in my
face
and her eyes smiling into mine,
when I so needed
that wild music
and that wild female willingness
to be
undone.

but they left me to sit alone
in tiny rented rooms
with only the company
of elderly landladies
and the comings and goings
of unsympathetic
roaches, they
left me terribly alone with
suicide mornings and
park bench
nights.

and now that
they are old
and
I am old

I don't want to know
them
now

or even to know
their
daughters

even though
the gods
in their infinite wisdom
still refuse to
let me
forget and
rest.

some personal thoughts

they're right: maybe it's been too easy just writing about myself and horses and drinking, but then I'm not trying to prove anything. taking long walks lately has been pleasant and although my desire for the female remains, I find that I needn't always be on the lookout for new conquests. riding the same mare need not be boring. let the wild young fillies be a problem for other men. I am often satisfied just being alone. I now find people more amusing than disgusting (am I weakening?) and although I still have nights and days of depression the typewriter does not fail me. readers expect continual growth from their poets but at this time just holding (the fort, haha) seems miraculous. long walks, yes. and the ability not to care—at times—as our society erupts and struggles does not mean that I am the victim of artistic loss. solitary evenings behind drawn blinds, being neither rich nor poor, can be satisfying. will madness arrive on schedule? I don't know and I don't seek an answer—just a small quiet space between not knowing, not wanting to know and finally finding out.

he's a dog

who? Chinaski? he hates fags and women.
he's a drunk. he beats his wife. he's a Nazi.
he only writes about sex and drinking. who
cares about that?
and he's a nasty drunk.
I don't understand what people see in his
writing.
I am the real genius and now
Chinaski has asked his publishers not to
publish me!
I've known some of the greatest writers
of our time!
Chinaski has met nobody.
I got him his start!
I got him included in that prestigious
anthology!
how does he repay me?
he writes unflattering things about
me.
and he claims he's lived with all
those beautiful women.
have you ever seen his face?
who would bed down a man
like that?
and he's had no education, no formal
training.
he has no idea what a stanza
is.
or for that matter—a line
break.
he just begins at the top

of the page and runs on to the
bottom.
and he says things like,
"Shakespeare bores me."
Shakespeare!
imagine that!
and the only people he cares to see
now are the Hollywood stars!
he doesn't want to see anybody
else.
well, I don't want to see him
either.
I remember when he lived
in rooms the size of a
closet.
now that he has had a few books
published
he's too good for the
rest of us!

look, I'm tired of talking about
Chinaski.
I want you to look at these
poems here.
my Collected Works,
my work of a lifetime.
I sent them to Chinaski for a
reading,
asked for a foreword or
at least a
blurb.

that was two months ago and
not a word from him
since.
not even a sign that
he's received the
stuff.

and I got him his start!
I got him in that prestigious anthology!
and then he asked his publishers not
to publish me!

tremor

at 9:50 the dogs started barking.
a few minutes later there was an earthquake
near Palm Springs.
the television stations break into their
programs with the news.
then the radio stations begin belaboring
the situation and
the earthquake experts at Caltech are
asked for their opinion.

the announcers are in their element.
phones begin to ring
in radio stations all
over the city.
yes, it was a quake.
yes, there will be aftershocks.
yes, we should check for gas leaks
and run a supply of water into the tub.
yes, we are all as one now.
yes, we have something we can all talk about
and we can talk about it
together.
yes, we should all call our friends
to be sure they're safe.
(I can only wonder,
will some say they were copulating when
it happened?
will others have been sitting on the
toilet?
so many people may have been copulating
or sitting on the toilet!)
the announcer continues:

what's that, caller?
you say you were copulating on the toilet
when it happened?
this is no time to be funny!
now we will switch to our Eye in the
Sky.
Henderson?
Henderson, are you there?
Henderson?
very well, ladies and gentlemen, we seem to have
lost contact with Henderson
so we'll go to our roving reporter who is now
on the scene.

Barbara, are you there?

my Mexican buddy

I liked him
he was clever and he could make me laugh
and often when he worked the case next to
mine we would stick our letters together and
talk
even though it was against the
rules.

he had become an American citizen
had found his way into the post office
and owned a movie theatre in
Mexico City.
I usually disliked ambitious fellows
but this guy was humorous so I forgave
him his ambition.

"hey, man," he asked me one night,
"how long has it been since you had
a piece of ass?"

"god, I don't know, man, 10 years
I guess."

"10 years? how old are you?"

"50."

"well, listen, I've been shacked with this
crazy woman, you know, and I've told her all
about you and I thought I might send her
over to your place some night, she could cook
you dinner or something. how about it?"

"please do not project your troubles
upon me," I told him.

"I didn't think it would work,"
he said with a grin.

the supervisor walked up behind us and
stood there.
"listen, I've warned you guys about
talking!"

"about talking when?" I asked.

"listen," he said, "just keep it up and I'll
fry your ass!"

"you win," I said.

the supervisor walked away.
interesting things like that happened there
almost every night!

strangers at the racetrack

I do not want to meet
them or
their wife
or look at
photographs of
their
children.

this is
serious business
this is
war
all
the
time.

I look into
their
maledict
eyes,
excuse myself
and walk
away.

and as
Rome burns and as
the odds
flash on the
tote board
Lady Luck
smiles,
crosses

her
legs
and
applauds
my
grit.

will you tiptoe through the tulips with me?

the sky is broken like a wet sack of
offal.
the air stinks, I walk into a building,
wait for the elevator, it arrives, I get in and
join 3 people with new shoes and
dead eyes.
we rise toward the tenth floor.
one of the people is a big woman
with long brown hair.
she begins to hum a little song.
I hate it.
I press the button and get off the
elevator 2 floors
early.
I wait for the next elevator.
it arrives.
it's empty.
it's a beautiful elevator.
I go up two floors, get out and
walk down the hall looking for
room 1002.
I find it.
I go in.
I tell the receptionist that I have a
2 o'clock appointment.
she tells me to be seated, that
they will be with me
soon.
I sit down.
there is only one other person in
the waiting room.
it is the big woman who was humming

the little song on the
elevator.
now she is silent.
she wears a green dress and
pretends to read a
magazine.
I look at her legs.
not good legs.
I get up and walk out, walk down
the hall.
I find a water fountain,
bend over, drink some
water.
then I walk back to
1002.
the woman in the green
dress is gone
but where she was
sitting on that chair
there is her green dress,
nicely folded, her shoes
and her panty
hose.
her purse is gone.
the receptionist slides
back the glass partition
and smiles at me:
"we'll be with you
soon!"
as she slides the
partition closed

I get up and walk out of there,
fast.
I take the elevator down.
soon I am at the first floor and
then I am outside on the
street.
as I walk away from the
building I look back.
flames are rising from
the windows of the tenth
floor and spreading up.
nobody on the street seems
to notice.
I decide to have lunch.
I look for a place to eat.
I walk along humming the
same little song that the big
woman hummed.
it's now about 95 degrees on a hot
Wednesday afternoon in
August
exactly one
year from
yesterday.

the novel life

one night I started
shivering, I got *ice cold*, I shivered and
shook for 2 and one half hours, the whole
bed jumped, it was like an
earthquake.

"you're panicking," said my girl. "breathe deeply
and try to relax."

"I'm not panicking," I said. "death doesn't
mean shit to me. this is coming from some
place that I don't understand."

all during the freezing and shaking,
my only thought was, well, I've written my 5th
novel but I haven't made the final revisions yet.
it's not fair that I die
now.

then I got well and revised my 5th novel and
it's supposed to be out next spring, so you
know I won't die, be killed, or catch a fatal
disease until then.

even in midlife I never
dreamed I'd write a novel
and here I've written 5, it's a bloody
miracle, a shout from the heart,
far from the school yards of hell

which started the luck
and far from
the world of hell that followed and
which kept it
going.

thanks for your help

here
there's less and less reason to write as they all close in.
I've barricaded the doors and windows, have bottled water, canned
food, candles, tools, rope, bandages, toothpicks, catnip,
mousetraps, reading material, toilet paper, blankets, firearms,
mirrors, knives
—cigarettes, cigars, candy—
memories, regrets, my birth certificate,
photographs of
picnics
parades
invasions;
I have roach spray, fine French wine, paper clips and last year's
calendar because
THIS COULD BE MY LAST POEM.
it could happen and, of course, I've considered and
reconsidered
d e a t h
but I haven't yet come up with *how,* which makes me feel
rather foolish about everything,
especially now.
—just waiting is the worst.
nothing worse than waiting
just waiting. always hated to
wait. what's there about waiting that's so
intolerable?
—like you're waiting for me to finish this
poem and
I don't know exactly
how
so I won't.

—so, if you happen to read this
in a magazine or a book
just
rip the page out
tear it up
and that's the graceful way
to end this poem
once and for
all.

I have continued regardless

almost ever since I began writing
decades ago
I have been dogged by
whisperers and gossips
who have proclaimed
daily
weekly
yearly
that
I can't write anymore
that now
I slip
and fall.

when I first began
there was much complaining about
the content of my
poems and stories.
"who cares about the low life of a
drunken bum?
is that all he can write about,
whores and puking?"

and now
their complaint is:
"who cares about the life of a
rich
bum?
why doesn't he write about whores
and puking
anymore?"

the Academics consider me
too raw
and I haven't consorted with most of the
others.

the few people I know well have nothing to do
with poetry.

there has also been envy-hatred
on the part of
some fellow writers
but I consider this
one of my finest
accomplishments.

when I first began this dangerous
game
I predicted that these
very things would
occur.

let them all rail:
if it wasn't me,
it would just be someone
else.

these
gossips and complainers,
what have *they* accomplished
anyway?

never having risen
they
can neither
slip nor
fall.

balloons

I saw too many faces today
faces like balloons.

at times I felt like
lifting the skin
and asking,
"anybody under there?"

there are medical terms for
fear of height
for
fear of
enclosed spaces.

there are medical terms for
any number of
maladies

so
there must be a medical term
for:
"too many people."

I've been stricken with
this malady
all my life:
there has always been
"too many people."

I saw too many faces
today, hundreds of
them

with eyes, ears, lips,
mouths, chins and so
forth

and
I've been alone
for several hours
now

and
I feel that I am
recovering.

which is the good part
but the problem
remains
that I know I'm going to
have to go out there
among them
again.

moving toward the dark

if we can't find the courage to go on,
what will we do?
what should we do?
what would you do?
if we can't find the courage to go on,
then
what day
what minute
in what year
did we go
wrong?
or was it an accumulation of all the
years?

I have some answers.
to die, yes.
to go mad, maybe.

or perhaps to
gamble everything away?

if we can't find the courage to go on,
what should we do?
what did all the others
do?

they went on
living their lives,
badly.

we'll do the same,
probably.

living too long
takes more than
time.

the real thing

yes, I know that you think
I am wrong
but
I know what is right for me
and what
is not.
may I tell you my
dream?

I am surrounded by
thick cement walls,
I am dressed in a red
robe
and I am sitting at an
organ.
there is
not a
sound.
I begin to play the
organ.
the hiss of the notes
is sharp and soft
at the same
time.

it is a slightly bitter
music
but among the dark notes
there are flashes of light and
laughter.

as I play,
the incomprehensible mystery
of the past
and of the present
becomes
comprehensible.

and best of all,
as I play,
nobody hears the music
but me.

the music is only for
me.

that is my
dream.

she looked at me and asked,

did you?

did you?

did you?

on the cuff

Jane would awaken early
(and 8:30 a.m. is early
when you go to bed at
dawn).

she would awaken crying and bitching
for a drink.

she'd keep at it, bitching and wailing,
just laying there flat on her back
and running all that noise
through my
hangover.

until finally, I'd leap out of bed
landing hard on my feet. "ALL RIGHT,
ALL RIGHT, GOD DAMN IT, SHUT UP!"

and I'd climb into the same pants, the
same shirt, the same dirty socks, I was
unshaven, unbrushed, young and mad—
mad, yes, to be shacked with a woman
ten years older than
I.

no job, behind in the rent, the same tired old
script.

down three flights of stairs and out
the back way
(the apartment house manager hung out
by the front entrance,

Mr. Notes-under-the-door, Mr.
Cop-caller, Mr. Listen-we-have-only-
nice-tenants-here).

then down the hill to the liquor
store around the corner, old Don Kaufman
who wired all the bottles
to the counter, even the cheap
stuff.

and Don would see me coming, "no, no,
not today!"

he meant no booze without
cash, I was into him pretty deep
but each time I looked at all
those bottles
I got angry because
he didn't need all those
bottles.

"Don, I want 3 bottles of cheap
wine."

"oh no, Hank."

he was an old man, I terrorized
him and part of me felt bad
doing it.
the old fart should have
blown me away
with his handgun.

"Hank, you used to be such a nice
man, such a gentleman.
what's happened?"

"look, Don, I don't want a character
analysis, I want 3 bottles of cheap
wine."

"when are you going to pay?"

"Don, I'm going to get an income tax
refund any day
now."

"I can't let you have anything,
Hank."

then I'd take hold of the counter
and begin rocking it, ripping at it,
the bottles rattling, joints and seams
giving way

all the while
cussing my ass
off.

"all right, Hank, *all
right!*"

then
back up the hill, back through
the rear entrance, up the three
flights of stairs

and there she'd be, still in bed.
she was getting fatter and
fatter, although we seldom
ate.

"3 bottles," I said, "of
port."

"thank god!"

"no, thank *me*. I work the
miracles around
here."

then
I'd pour the port into
two tall water
glasses

another day
begun.

alone again

I think of each of
them
living somewhere else
sitting somewhere else
standing somewhere else
sleeping somewhere else
or maybe feeding a
child
or
reading a
newspaper or screaming
at their
new man . . .

but thankfully
my female past
(for me)
has concluded
peacefully.

yet most others seem to
believe that a
new relationship will certainly
work.

that the last one
was simply the
error of
choosing a bad
mate.

just
bad taste
bad luck
bad fate.

and then there are some who
believe that old
relationships can be
revived and made new
again.

but please
if you feel that way

don't phone
don't write
don't arrive

and meanwhile,
don't
feel bruised because this
poem will last much
longer than we
did.

it deserves to:
you see
its strength is
that it seeks
no
mate at
all.

fooling Marie (the poem)

he met her at the racetrack, a strawberry
blonde with round hips, well-bosomed, long legs,
turned-up nose, flower mouth, in a pink dress,
wearing white high-heeled shoes.
she began asking him questions about various
horses while looking up at him with her pale blue
eyes.

he suggested the bar and they had a drink, then
watched the next race together.
he hit fifty-win on a sixty-to-one shot and she
jumped up and down.
then she whispered in his ear,
"you're the magic man! I want to fuck you!"
he grinned and said, "I'd like to, but
Marie . . . my wife . . ."
she laughed, "we'll go to a motel!"

so they cashed the ticket, went to the parking lot,
got into her car. "I'll drive you back when
we're finished," she smiled.

they found a motel about a mile
west. she parked, they got out, checked in, went to
room 302.
they had stopped for a bottle of Jack Daniel's
on the way. he stood and took the glasses out of the
cellophane. as she undressed he poured two.

she had a marvelous young body. she sat on the edge of
the bed sipping at the Jack Daniel's as he
undressed. he felt awkward, fat and old

but knew he was lucky: it promised to be his best day
ever.
then he too sat on the edge of the bed with her and
his Jack Daniel's. she reached over
and grabbed him between the legs, bent over
and went down on him.

he pulled her under the covers and they played some more.
finally, he mounted her and it was great, it was a
miracle, but soon it ended, and when she
went to the bathroom he poured two more drinks
thinking, I'll shower real good, Marie will never
know.

she came out and they sat in bed
making small talk.
"I'm going to shower now," he told her,
"I'll be out soon."

"o.k., cutie," she said.

he soaped good in the shower, washing away all the
perfume, the woman-smell.

"hurry up, daddy!" he heard her say.

"I won't be long, baby!" he yelled from the
shower.

he got out, toweled off, then opened the bathroom
door and stepped out.

the motel room was empty.
she was gone.

on some impulse he ran to the closet, pulled the door
open: nothing there but coat hangers.

then he noticed that his clothes were gone, his under-
wear, his shirt, his pants with the car keys and his wallet,
all the money, his shoes, his stockings, everything.

on another impulse he looked under the bed.
nothing.

then he saw the bottle of Jack Daniel's, half full,
standing on the dresser.
he walked over and poured a drink.
as he did he saw the word scrawled on the dresser
mirror in pink lipstick: SUCKER.

he drank the whiskey, put the glass down and watched himself
in the mirror, very fat, very tired, very old.
he had no idea what to do next.

he carried the whiskey back to the bed, sat down,
lifted the bottle and sucked at it as the light from the
boulevard came in through the dusty blinds. then he just sat
and looked out and watched the cars, passing back and
forth.

the copulation blues

fuck
the phone rings once
stops
fuck
I am on top
we roll off to the side
fuck
she throws one leg over
and plays with her clit
while I harpoon her
fuck
the dog scratches on the door
won't stop
I get up and let him in
then it's time to
suck
she's got it in her mouth
not the dog
me
suck suck
the doorbell rings
a man selling mops made by the blind
we buy a mop for eleven dollars with a little gadget
that squeezes out the water
fuck
now it's up again
I'm on top again
the phone rings
a girlfriend of hers from Stockton

they talk for ten minutes
finish
I am reading the sports section when
she comes back with a bowl of grapes and
I hand her the woman's page
no fuck.

the faithful wife

she was a married woman
and she wrote sad
and futile poems
about her married life.
her many letters to me
were the same: sad
and repetitive and
futile.

we exchanged letters for
some years.
I was depressed and suicidal
and had had nothing but
bad luck
with women
so I continued to write
her
thinking, well, maybe
this way
no ill will come to
either one of us.

but
one night suddenly
she was in town, she
phoned me:
"I'm at a meeting of
The Chaparral Poets of
California!"

"o.k.," I said, "good
luck."

"I mean," she asked,
"don't you want to
see me?"

"oh, yeah . . ."

she told me she would be
waiting at a certain bar
in Pasadena.

I had half a glass of
whiskey, 2 cans of beer
and
set out.

I found the bar, went
in.
there she was (she had
sent photos) the little
housewife giddy on
martinis.
I sat down beside
her.

"oh my god," she said, "it's *you*!
I just can't believe it!"

I ordered a couple of drinks from
the barkeep.

she kissed me right there, tongue
and all.

we had a couple more drinks
then got into my car
and with her
holding my cock
I drove the freeway
back to my place
where I sat her down.
she began talking about
poetry
but I got her back
into the bedroom
got her down onto the bed
and stripped down
except for the
panties.
I had never seen
such a
beautiful body.

I began to slip the
panties off but she
said, "no, no, I can TELL
you're very POTENT, you'll make
me PREGNANT!"

"well," I said, "what the hell!"

I rolled over then and went to
sleep.

the next morning
I drove her back to her
Chaparral Poets of
California.

as the weeks and months
went on
her letters kept arriving.
I answered some, then
stopped.

but her letters kept coming.
there wasn't much news
but many photos: photos of
her children, photos of her,
there was one photo of her
sitting alone on a rock
by the seashore.

then the letters were fewer and
fewer and then they stopped.

add some years
some other women
many changes of address
and one day
a new letter found
its way to
me:

the children were grown
and gone.
her husband had lost his
part of the business, his
partners had knifed
him,
they were going to have to
sell the house.

I answered that
letter.

two or three weeks
passed.
her next letter said
that there was a divorce and
it was final.
she enclosed a photo.
I didn't know who it
was at first.
182 pounds. she said
she'd been living on
submarine sandwiches and
refried beans and was
looking for a job.
never had a job.
she could only type
23 w.p.m.
she enclosed a small
chapbook of her poems
inscribed "Love."

I should have fucked her that
long-ago night.
I should have been a
dog.

it would have been one good
night for each of us, especially
for me
stuck between suicide and
insanity
in bed with the beautiful
housewife.
I had never seen a body like
hers before.

now I don't even have
her letters.
there are nearly a hundred
of them
somewhere

and this is
a sad futile poem
about it
all.

once in a while

it is only
once in a while
that you see
someone whose
electricity
and presence
matches yours
at that
moment

and then
usually it's
a stranger.

it was 3 or 4
years ago
I was walking on
Sunset Boulevard
toward Vermont
when
a block away
I noticed a
figure moving
toward me.

there was something
in her carriage
and in her walk
which
attracted
me.

as we came
closer
the intensity
increased.

suddenly
I knew her
entire history:
she had lived
all her life
with men
who had never really
known her.

as she approached
I became almost
dizzy.

I could hear her
footsteps as
she approached.

I looked into
her face.

she was as
beautiful
as I had
imagined she
would be.

as we passed
our eyes fucked
and loved and
sang to each
other

and then
she moved
past me.

I walked on
not looking
back.

then
when I looked
back
she was
gone.

what is one
to do
in a world
where almost everything
worth having
or doing
is
impossible?

I went into
a coffee shop
and decided that
if I ever saw
her again somehow
I'd say,
"listen, please,
I just *must*
speak to
you . . ."

I never saw her
again

I never will.

the iron in our
society silences
a man's
heart

and when you
silence a man's
heart
you leave him
finally
with only
a cock.

another high-roller

I went to Vegas last weekend
I had on that blue dress
low-cut and short
the one you like
and I wore my brown boots
and this guy at the crap table
he kept winning
and he kept feeding me chips
he said I brought him luck.
I won a few hundred but
I swear to Christ he must have
won 40 thousand dollars that
night.
he was a great guy.
he told me,
"don't go away, we're going to win
the *world!*"
it was some night, believe me.
I'll never forget it.
you don't like Vegas, do
you? she asked.

I once got married there,
I said.

and what did you do over the
weekend? she asked.

I waxed my car,
I told her.

the fucking horses

"the fucking horses," she said, "you keep bringing me
out to these fucking horse races and I lose, god damn it,
it's all so useless and ignorant, I hate it, I just
hate it!"

her purse had a long strap and she was swinging it
around and around with great velocity.

we were walking out of the track after the
last race.

"I told you," I said, "not to bet the horses with
high speed ratings, especially at comparative
distances."

"but shit," she screamed, "why *doesn't* it work?
the horse that ran faster last time, why doesn't
he win against the slower ones?"

"anybody can take a short price on exposed form,"
I said. "it's self-defeating."

"goddamn you!" she screamed. "I hate you and I hate horses!"

and she swung her purse around and around on its
long strap.

then there was a hard harsh thud:
she had just hit the man on the head
who was walking behind us.

the poor soul was badly staggered.
an elderly Mexican.

I held him up by the arm.

"I'm sorry, I'm sorry," I said,
"it was an accident!
she didn't mean to hit you with her
purse!
she has lost a great deal of money today
and she's a little crazy!
I'm very sorry!"

"it's all right," the fellow said.

I let go of his arm and we turned and
walked on.

"what's the matter?" she screamed.
"are you afraid of that man?
are you afraid of a real fight?"

"of course I am," I told her.

"I thought so!" she screamed. "let's
get the hell out of here!"

it was when we got to the car
and after I got it started that
this thought
went through my mind:
*baby, I don't know why the hell
I'm living with you!*

I stopped at the first light.
then as we drove up Huntington Drive
she said to me,
*"you know, I don't know why the hell
I'm living with you!"*

I kept on driving up Huntington.
then I turned on the car radio.
we had been together one and one-
half years.
it's always easier to meet than
to part.

I know
because after that day at the track
we managed to live together for another
year.

hello there!

when death comes with its last cold kiss
I'll be ready.
(I've already experienced my share of
deathly
kisses.)
the mad ladies who helped me
consume my hours
my years
have readied me for the
dark.

when death comes with its last cold kiss
I'll be ready:
just another whore
come to
shake me
down.

the fuck-master

Arnie was ahead of all of us, he began shaving
first and then he flashed rubbers at us
in their mysterious tin cases
and he was the first one with his own automobile
and he always had some girl in his
car, always a new one,
sitting there quiet and frightened
and we *knew* he was fucking her
and
he knew where to get gin, he'd get them
drunk on gin and then he'd do it to
them!

all that was in jr. high
but when we went on to
high school
Arnie kept going back to jr. high
to pick up the jr. high school girls
in his car (it was almost like he was stuck
back there in jr.
high).
well, time passed and then Arnie
dropped out of high school and
I forgot about
him.

two years later I was walking
home after classes one afternoon
and here came
Arnie.
Christ, he looked all *wizened,* almost
vanished.

I had gotten bigger and wiser meanwhile
and I was more comfortable with
things.

I slapped him on the back, "hey, Arnie, you
FUCKER, how ya
doin'?"

"hi, Hank," he
said.

we shook hands and his hand was trembling
and sweaty.

I let go of
it.

we stood and looked at each other.

"well, see you around, cousin," I
said.

and I
left him standing there.

the poor guy had fucked himself away, completely
fucked himself
away.

and I still had all mine
left!

my personal psychologist

you're a screwed-up Romantic, she said,
you read all the old philosophers and you
listen to Wagner and Mahler and you think
the ancient Chinese poets were hot shit, yet
you're depraved, you're at the racetrack
every day and you know that's sick, and
all that wine you drink, it's eating
your brain away, and when you get drunk
you talk about what a great fighter you
used to be, even though you admit you
took more beatings than you gave.
you dislike people and love animals.
I really don't know what the hell you're
all about—you just *grab* at things, you rely
solely on instinct and your prejudices
and sometimes I think you're *retarded.*
it was your childhood, you didn't get any
love so it's hard for you to give any,
you just get drunk and call every woman a
whore.

listen, I said, isn't there any more
beer?
and where the hell are the cigarettes?
there were 3 on this table a moment ago and
now they're all
gone!

jealousy

I know this fellow, he is
amazing, so terribly
dull
but get him in a room full of
women
and he will find the easy
one
and they will begin
talking
and eventually they will
vanish
and they will
fuck.

his conversation is quite
banal:
"oh, did your mother
come from Michigan? I had a
brother who went to the
University of Detroit!"

what all this means is
that he will talk and talk
about anything and listen and
listen forever to
everything.

the ladies really
ate
it
up.

most of us are
unable to accomplish
this kind of thing
but this fellow
can talk
dumb crap for hours
and much later
after completing his
coitus
he will walk in
with the smiling lady
like a Lion King
as if the
whole thing
was
an endearing adventure
and somehow
fulfilling
for us
all.

her guy

you had gotten out of
jail earlier that morning.
you got home about 4:30 a.m.
and started drinking with those
two dykes.
when I got there around 9 a.m.
you were lying on the couch with them
in your shorts and
undershirt
smoking an old cigar
and holding a beer can in your
hand,
you were a mess,
you had pennies and beer caps
stuck to your back
and the floor was covered with
bottles.

"hi, kid," you said,
"I just got out . . . we're celebrating."

you were totally gone.
I'd heard some terrible things about you
and finally
I believed them.

dead poet's wife

she told me that I was insensitive
that I didn't revere God or love
animals. even flies have souls,
she told me.

we were in a motel room at Laguna
Beach. she was overweight and
so was I and maybe in the
great all-encompassing nature of things
we both had souls
like flies.

I lifted my drink
and emptied it.

"shit," she said, "William drank too much
too. don't you know that life can be
beautiful?"

"yes, that's why I drink."

"don't you love the beauty of nature?" she
asked. "don't you ever think of the miracle
of birth?"

"I think of the miracle of death."

"I used to think you were a great poet,"
she said, "but now that I've met you and
know you better, I don't think that anymore.
you can't fuck
me."

"I don't have the desire to fuck
you," I answered, "and you know it."

it was 3 a.m. and I walked out of the
motel room with a new drink in my hand.
I was dressed in my shorts and I
finished the drink and dropped myself
into the swimming pool. all the lights
were out. the manager stepped out as
I dog-paddled about in the dark.

"what the hell are you doing?" he
screamed.
"turn on the pool lights," I screamed back.

the lights came on and I paddled around for
5 minutes more, then climbed out and walked
back into the motel room.

she had her back turned to me in the bed.
I got in with a new drink and looked at
my feet sticking out from under the covers.
I decided that I had the most beautiful feet
of any man on earth.
then the pool lights went out and all I
could see was the glowing end of my cigarette.
I decided that in the great all-encompassing
nature of things it must certainly have
a soul too.

scrambled legs

we were having lunch
at Hal's Diner.
"you know," he told me, "after we made love
the last time
she lay in my arms and cried. she said,
'oh my god, I miss him so!'
she was talking about you, Hank."

ıe way it is, Jack, with all
while I'm with them they hate
I leave them they love

ıpted to go back to them, however, I don't even

nd that I slept with her,

ou a good breakfast afterwards,

mber."

"well, I'll tell you: she didn't."

"is that the reason you left her:
because she couldn't cook
a good breakfast?"

"I never eat breakfast, Jack."

"then what happened?"

"too often, after we made love, she
began crying in my arms about how she
missed some other guy."

"well," he said, "I'll be a son-of-a-bitch."

"don't be," I said, "just pass the salt and
pepper."

endless love

I've seen old married couples
sitting in their rockers
across from one another
being congratulated
for staying together 60 or 70
years,
either of whom
would
long ago have
settled for something
else, anything else,
but fate
fear and
circumstances have
bound them
eternally together;
and as we tell them
how wonderful
their great and enduring love
is
only they
really know
the truth
but they don't tell us
that from the first day they
met
somehow
it didn't mean
all that much:

like
waiting for death
now
it was just an endless determination to
endure.

down and out on the boardwalk

she lived in Venice
on some 2nd floor
and I'd knock and she'd
let me in
and there was no bed
just a mat on the floor
and candles
everywhere
there was even a
piano
and there was also a
guitar
and while we sipped
white wine
she'd sit on the
floor
and play the
guitar
and sing songs
her own lyrics
godawful stuff
about the
soul
and I'd go to the
window
and look out and
say
"nice view but let's
work out."

"work out?"
she'd ask. "what
do you mean?"

"I mean
I'll suck your tits
and stuff."

"I want you to hear
this new
song."

she'd start right
in.

she had an awful
voice but
nice long
hair.

I'd get playful
and hammer on the
piano
just so I wouldn't
have to listen
to
her.

I was in a bad
way: in between
real women

and just
doing time
with
her.

one night I
asked her,
"listen, how do you
make it?"

"make it?"

"I mean
how do you pay the
rent, all
that?"

"oh, I'm a marriage
counselor."

"really?"

"yes."

"you been married?"

"3 times."

I finally stopped going
to her
place
but somehow
she found out where
I lived
and then came
to see
me.

she said we couldn't have
sex
because she was going to
be married again
and didn't want to be
untrue
to him.

she described
her boyfriend
in detail
to me
then took out her
guitar
and started
singing.

later that night
I sodomized her
and told her

not to
come
around any
more.

I got lucky:
she
didn't.

soon after that
I met a plump
Jewish girl
who promised
she'd
save me from
myself.

I thought
that would be
a very good
idea.

sex sister

there were 4 of them between the ages of 30 and 45 and
all they talked about was men and sex, I mean,
it was all-consuming, to them there wasn't anything
else.

I was living with the youngest sister and she had me
performing sexual acts I had never even heard of
before.

"now, let's try this."

"all right."

at first it was lively, adventurous, even
humorous
but
as the months passed and the nights added up I
began to resent it, like—oh, here we go with SEX
again!
(she also liked to do it in strange places like public
parks or in automobiles while I was driving.)

I began to feel that all the sisters were crazy; in fact,
one of them had been in a madhouse (the one I was with).

the sisters had boisterous, screeching laughs, really
rather ugly laughs
and I began drinking more so I could tolerate
them and their laughter.

the drinking made the sister I was with quite angry
because sometimes I would just go to sleep
instead of performing.

I finally told my lady that I couldn't take it anymore
and that it was over and she seemed to accept that at first
but finally it was not to be so:
she began to phone me continually, mostly at night,
around 3 or 4 a.m.: "YOU'VE GOT SOMEBODY THERE,
HAVEN'T YOU?"

she followed me everywhere. once I took some clothes in
to the cleaners and when I came out my car was nearly
destroyed—ripped upholstery, shattered windows, torn
dashboard, all within 3 or 4 minutes.
it looked as if a tiger had been in the car.

another time I was making love to another lady when my
bedroom window was
smashed open and there was the sister's face, twisted, spitting
at me, "YOU FUCKING BASTARD!" then she was
gone.

the lady in bed was terrified, trembling. "what was
that?"

"nothing, baby, nothing."

the sex sister also tried to murder me a couple of times in a couple
of different ways and just missed both
times.
let me tell you that the police weren't much
help, they picked her up but she somehow convinced
them that I was at fault.

"there's nothing wrong with that lady," they told me,
both times.

two squads of officers.

maybe she had sex with the whole gang of
them?

fortunately, as the months went on she gradually abandoned her
terrorist attacks until finally it was just a weepy
phone call or two and then a letter or two, then
silence.

she probably found somebody who could perform all the tricks that
she had taught me and could probably perform them
better. I hope
so.

and I just hope he likes sex
62 times a
month.

to the ladies no longer here

it's just as well

you should see me now

driving to the racetrack

a tiny German flag decorating the rear
window.

I dislike the heavy traffic on the
boulevard and
I drive through the back streets of the black
ghetto.

the years have gone by
quickly.

Death sits in the seat next to
me.

we make a lovely
couple.

a man finds consolation while driving
and waiting.

one consolation is
how lucky I am
that I never settled down permanently
with any one of the
ladies.

driving along, that thought comes back to
me and falls at my feet.

Death picks it up
looks at me
shudders
and quickly fastens his
seat belt.

the nude dancer

she's got a 6-month-old baby
and a 9-year-old
son,
but
she said
it sure beats the factories.

why do those guys just sit there and
stare at that thing
when a woman's dancing? I
asked.

they memorize it, she said, then they
go home and flog off. I danced last
night and nobody watched me.
they were all watching some movie
where this woman was fingering
herself, and
after I finished my dance
I stood there and told them,
you guys are going to go crazy watching that
shit. you don't know where you're at
anymore.

you know, some of those guys freaked
out? about 7 of them got up and
left.

no shit, I said.

no shit, she said. I've worked 3 different places
since I've seen you
last. but it beats the factories and
it beats the
streets.
at least you can catch a drink
once in a while.

yes, that's right,
I told her,
that's right.

Ma Barker loves me

lying in the sack in the dark
sick from days of drinking.

head hurting
tongue thick.

watching tv
phone off the hook.

tired of trying to relate to the
female,
I watch tv.

the walls stacked up around me
like shields.

I watch these guys blasting holes
in people
with their submachineguns.

they need money
they have trouble with their molls
things keep
screwing up.

I get up to piss during a tire
commercial.

when I get back the main guy is
lying out in a field with his
moll.

there's a stream below them.

it's peaceful but he has a cigar
stuck into his mouth and a .357 magnum
resting in his shoulder holster.

the moll leans over him
she has blonde wispy hair which flicks
in the wind.

she says, "Johnny, why don't you give
it up?"

"give *what* up?" he asks.

"you know, Johnny," she says, "killing
people and all that . . ."

"now, baby," he says, "I'm just trying
to get by."

"you could give all that up, Johnny, we
could settle down in a nice little place
with a picket fence and have babies . . ."

"ah, now, baby, that life ain't for
me."

"well, Johnny," she smiles, "it's either
give it up or lose me . . ."

he sits up
pushes her away:

"no, baby! you don't *mean* that?"

"yes," she says, "I *do*, Johnny!"

"I'm not going to live without you,
baby," he says

takes out the .357
jams it between her legs and
pulls the trigger.

I get up
go to the refrigerator and
get a beer.

when I come back
there's a shaving cream commercial
on.

I drain the beer
toss it in the basket
put the phone back on the hook
dial a number.

she answers and I say, "listen,
baby, I can't have you around
anymore, you
get in the way.
sorry."

I hang up
take the phone back
off the hook.

time for another beer.

I like gangster movies
best.

here we go again

it's stupid, I know, but I have an
ability to feel happy for little or no reason,
it's not a great elation, it's
more like a steady
warmth—
something like a warm heater on a cold
night.

I have no religion, and not even a
decent philosophy
and I'm not
stupid: I know that death will finally
arrive
but don't consider even this to be
a negative
factor.

which is to say that in spite of
everything, I feel good
most of the
time.

I appear to handle setbacks, bad
luck, minor tragedies, without
difficulty, my mood remains
unchanged.
much experience, perhaps, has taught
me
how to remain unmoved.

yet there is one situation
I can't endure:
a bitter, depressed, angry
woman
can still murder any
good feelings
that I might have—and
just like that I despair and
fall into a black
pit.
this occurs with some
regularity and unfortunately
in the wink of an
eye I am sullen and
depressed.

and that's stupid,
I should be able to ignore
female
disorders
even as the dark shit
(that despite the dark shit)
floods my
brain.

do you believe that a man can be taught to write?

there was my cheap hotel; I was up on the 4th floor; I'd
bring a lady in from the bar 2 or 3 times a week and we'd burst into that
lobby like we wanted to wreck something, and the desk clerk, a really
nice fellow, was terrified of me, I was big of chest and gut and when
the writing was going badly, which it often was, upon
entering with my lady, I'd take it out on the desk clerk: "hey,
buddy, I think I'll take one of your legs, twist it up the middle
of your back and wind you like a clock!"
I had him so scared he only called the cops once or twice and I
had fun with the cops—barricading the door and listening to the dumb
useless double-talk that cops liked to use; I always wore them
down and they never got in.

up there I stripped to my undershirt and shorts, I was nuts,
had very muscular legs, strutted up and down the room saying, "look at
my legs, baby! you ever seen legs like that?"

I always pretended to be the toughest guy in town but
when it actually came to fighting I wasn't all that good: I
could take a hell of a punch and didn't have much fear but my own left
hook and right cross were missing, and worse, I couldn't seem to
get the hatred going, it all seemed a joke to me, even when some guy was
crushing my head against the edge of some urinal.
but let's forget all that! up on that 4th floor, I was best, the red neon
sign near the downtown library flashing CHRIST SAVES, me
strutting about and proclaiming, "nobody knows I'm a genius but
me!"
and all the time I was strutting I would glance over at my lady of
the night, looking at those legs, those high heels, thinking, I'm going
to rip the love out of those high-heeled shoes and those ankles and those
thighs and that dumb pitiful face, I'm going to make her come alive!

and poor Hemingway, I thought, never met dolls like I've met dolls!

which was true.

he would have walked away.

hail and farewell

as gentle as a butterfly
fluttering in the
murdered light
you came through here
like fire singing
and when it was over
the walls came down
the flags went up
and love was finished.

you left behind a pair of shoes
an old purse
and some birthday and
Xmas cards
from me all
held together
by a green rubber
band.

all well and good enough,
I suppose,
because
when your lover is gone,
thank the gods,
the silence is
final.

weep

weep for the indifference of flying fish

weep for the absence of long-haired blondes

weep for the sadness of yourself

weep for Bach

weep for the extinct animals

weep for grandfather's clock

weep for weeping
because no one cares

the doors open in and out
the lights go on and off
teeth are pulled

I forgive the indifference of flying fish

I forgive the butterfly and the moth

I forgive the first woman who held my psyche
in her fingertips when

I was sold into captivity
long ago.

it's a lonely world

of frightened people.

a note upon modern poesy

poetry *has* come a long way, though very slowly;
you aren't as old as I am
and I can remember reading
magazines where at the end of a poem
it said:
Paris, 1928.
that seemed to make a
difference, and so, those who could afford to
(and some who couldn't)
went to
PARIS
and wrote.

I am also old enough so that I remember when poems
made many references to the Greek and Roman
gods.
if you didn't know your gods you weren't a very good
writer.
also, if you couldn't slip in a line of
Spanish, French or
Italian,
you *certainly* weren't a very good
writer.

5 or 6 decades ago,
maybe 7,
some poets started using
"i" for "I"
or
"&" for "and."

many still use a small
"i" and many more continue to use the
"&"
feeling that this is
poetically quite effective and
up-to-date.

also, the oldest notion still in vogue is
that if you can't understand a poem then
it almost certainly is a
good one.

poetry is still moving slowly forward, I guess,
and when your average garage mechanics
start bringing books of poesy to read
on their lunch breaks
then we'll know for sure we're moving in
the right
direction.

&
of this
i
am sure.

the end of an era

he lived in the Village
in New York
in the old days
and only after he died
did he get a write-up
in a snob magazine,
a magazine which had
never printed his
poems.

he came from the days
when poets called
themselves
Bohemians.
he wore a beret and a
scarf
and hung around the
cafés,
bummed drinks,
sometimes got a
night's lodging from the
rich
(just for
laughs)
but mostly
he slept in the alleys
at night.
the whores knew him
well
and gave him
little
hand-outs.

he was a communist
or a
socialist
depending upon what
he was
reading
at that
moment.

it was 1939
and he had a
burning hatred
in his heart
for the
Nazis.

when he
recited his poems
in the street
he always
ended up
frothing about the
Nazis.

he passed out
little stapled
pages
of his
poems
and
he wrote

with a
simple
intensity.

he was good
but not
great.

and even the good poems
were not
that
good.

anyhow
he was an
attraction;
the tourists always
asked for
him.

he was always
in love
with some
new whore.

he had a
real
soul
and the usual
real
needs.

he stank
and wore cast-off clothes
and he screamed
when he spoke
but
at least
he wasn't anybody
but
himself.

the Village was
his
Paris.
but unlike
Henry Miller
who made
failure
glorious
and finally
lucrative
he didn't know
quite how
to accomplish
that.

instead of being
a
genius-freak
he was just
a
freak-freak.

but most of
the writers and
painters
who also had failed
loved him
because he
symbolized
for them
the possibility
of being
recognized.
they too wore
scarves and
berets
and did more
complaining than
creating.

but then they
lost him.

he was found
one morning
in an
alley
wrapped around
his latest
whore.

both of them
had their
throats
cut
wide.

and
on the wall
above them
in their
blood
were scrawled
the words:
"COMMIE PIG!"

another freak
had found
him?
a
freak-Nazi?
or maybe
just a
freak-freak?

but his
murder
finally created
the fame
he had always
wanted,
though it was

to be but
temporary.

he was to
have a
final
fling
in this
his
crazy
life and
death.

he had left
an envelope
with a prominent
Matron of the
Arts,
marked:
TO BE OPENED
ONLY IN THE EVENT
OF
MY DEATH.

all during his
stay in the
Village
he had spoken
about a mysterious
WORK IN
PROGRESS.

he had claimed
he'd written a
GIGANTIC WORK,
more pages than
a couple of
telephone
books.
it would
dwarf Pound's
Cantos
and put a
headlock
on the
Bible.

the instructions
were
specific:
the WORK was
in an iron
chest
buried
in a graveyard
30 yards
south and west
of a certain tree
(indicated on a
hand-drawn
map)
the tree
where he claimed
Whitman once

rested
while he wrote
"I Celebrate Myself."

the ground
all about was
soon
dug up and
searched.

nothing was
found.

some Romantics
claimed it was
still
there
somewhere.

Realists
claimed it never had
been there.

maybe the
Nazis
got there
first?

at any rate
it was
shortly after
that

that
almost all the
poets
in the
Village

and most poets
living
elsewhere

stopped
wearing
scarves and
berets
and reluctantly
went off to
war.

Paris in the spring

if death was staring you in the face,
he was asked, what would you say to your readers?
nothing, he told the interviewer, would you please
order another bottle of wine?
he was an old, tired writer from Los Angeles, hungover,
and his French publisher had pushed one more
interview on him.

the free dinners and drinks usually
were great
but now he was fed up.
the many recent interviews had become
frustrating and boring.
he figured either his books would sell on their own
or fail the same way.
he hadn't written them for money anyhow but to keep
himself out of the madhouse.
he tried to tell the interviewers this but they just went on with their usual
banal questions:
have you met Norman Mailer?
what do you think of Camus, Sartre, Céline?
do your books sell better here than in America?
did you really work in a slaughterhouse?
do you think Hemingway was homosexual?
do you take drugs?
do you drink when you write?
are you a misanthrope?
who is your favorite writer?

the interviewer ordered another bottle of wine.
it was 11:15 p.m. on the patio of a hotel.
there were little white tables and chairs scattered about.

theirs was the only one occupied.
there was the interviewer, a photographer,
the writer and his wife.

have you had sex with children? the interviewer
asked.
no, answered the writer.
in one of your stories a man has sex with a
child and you describe it very
graphically.
well? asked the writer.
it was as if you enjoyed it, the interviewer said.
I sometimes enjoy writing, the writer said.
you seemed to have experienced what you were describing,
said the interviewer.
I only photograph life, said the writer. I might write
about a murderer but this doesn't mean that I am
one or would enjoy being one.

ah, here's the wine, said the interviewer.
the waiter took out the cork, poured a bit for
him.
the interviewer took a taste, nodded to the
waiter
and the waiter poured all
around.

the wine goes fast when there's four of us, said the
writer.

do you drink because you are afraid of life?
the interviewer asked.

disgusted with life is more like it, said the writer, *and with you.*

we were up very early, said the writer's wife.
he's given at least a dozen interviews over the past
3 days and he's tired.

I am from one of the city's most important newspapers,
said the interviewer.

fuck you, said the writer.

what? said the interviewer. you can't talk to me
like that!

I am, said the writer.

all you American writers think you're God, said the
interviewer.

God is dead, said the writer, remember?

this interview is over! said the interviewer.

the photographer quickly drank his wine,
then he and the interviewer stood up
and walked out.

you better get yourself together, said the wife
to the writer, you're on television tomorrow
night.

I'll tell them to kiss my ass, said the writer.

you can't do that, said his wife.

baby, said the writer, lifting his
wineglass, watch me!

you're just a drunk who writes, said his wife.

that's better than a drunk who just drinks,
said the writer.

his wife sighed.
well, do you want to go back to the room or to another
café?

to another café, said the writer.

they rose and walked slowly out of the
restaurant, he looking through his pocket for
cigarettes, she looking back over her shoulder
as if something was following
them.

alone in this chair

hell, hell, in hell,
trapped like a fish to bake
here and burn.
hell, hell, inside my brain
inside my gut,
hell hanging
twisting
screaming
churning
then crouching still
both inside
and outside of
me.
hell,
hell in the trees,
on the ground,
crawling on the rug.
hell,
bouncing off
the
walls and
ceiling as
I sit in this chair here
as outside
through the window
I watch
6 or 7 telephone wires
taut against the
sky
as fresh hell slides
toward me
along the wires.

hell is where I
am.
and I am
here.

there isn't any
place
else.

see me now
reaching for a
cigarette,
my hand pushing
through boiling space.

there is nothing more
I can do.

I light the
cigarette,
lean back here
alone
in
this
chair.

talking about the poets

"correctly so," I told him,
"I would much rather they all
robbed banks or sold
drugs and if you please may
I have a vodka-
7?"

"I agree," said the
barkeep mixing the
drink, "I'd rather they
collected garbage
or ran for Congress
or taught
biology."

"or," I said, reaching
for the drink, "sold
flowers on the corner
or gave back rubs or
tried blowing glass."

"absolutely right," said
the barkeep
pouring himself a
drink, "I'd rather they
plowed the good
earth or
delivered the mail."

"or," I said, "mugged
old ladies or
pulled teeth."

"or directed traffic or
worked the factories,"
said the barkeep, "or
caught the bus to
the nearest harvest."

"that will be a great day," I said,
"when it arrives."

"beautiful," said the
barkeep, "but isn't it the
mediocrity of the masses
which diminishes the
wealth of its entertainers
and artists?"

"absolutely not," I said, "and may I
have another vodka-7?"

"if I was the policeman
of the world," the barkeep
continued, moving the drink
toward me, "many a darling
poet would either be allowed to
starve or forced to get a
real job."

"and correctly so," I
said, raising my
drink.

"that will be a beautiful day,"
said the barkeep,
"when it arrives."

"a hell of a beautiful
day," I agreed.

was Li Po wrong?

you know what Li Po said when asked if he'd rather be an
Artist or Rich?
"I'd rather be Rich," he replied, "for Artists can usually be found
sitting on the doorsteps of the
Rich."
I've sat on the doorsteps of some expensive and
unbelievable homes
myself
but somehow I always managed to disgrace myself and / or insult
my Rich hosts
(mostly after drinking large quantities of their fine
liquor).
perhaps I was afraid of the Rich?
all I knew then was poverty and the very poor,
and I felt instinctively that the Rich shouldn't be so
Rich,
that it was some kind of clever
twist of fate
based on something rotten and
unfair.
of course, one could say the same thing
about being poor,
only there were so many poor, it all seemed completely
out of proportion.
and so when I, as an Artist, visited the
homes of the Rich, I felt ashamed to be
there, and I drank too much of their fine wines,
broke their expensive glassware and antique dishes,
burned cigarette holes in their Persian rugs and
mauled their wives,
reacting badly to the whole damned
situation.

yet I had no political or social solution.
I was just a lousy houseguest,
I guess,
and after a while
I protected both myself and the Rich
by rejecting their
invitations
and everybody felt much better after
that.
I went back to
drinking alone,
breaking my own cheap glassware,
filling the room with cigar
smoke and feeling
wonderful
instead of feeling trapped,
used,
pissed on,
fucked.

operator

the phone doesn't ring.
the hours hang limp and empty.
everybody else is having it
all.

it seems to never end.

one night it got very bad.
I needed just a voice.

I dialed the time on the
telephone and listened to her
voice as she said:

"it's eleven ten and ten seconds.
it's eleven ten and twenty seconds.
it's eleven ten and thirty seconds . . ."

then she told me that it
was:
"eleven ten and forty seconds."

she might have saved my life
although I'm not sure.

a note from Hades in the mailbox

it reads:
Mr. Chinaski, we stopped by to see if
you're interested in a free lunch.
we'll stop by again later this
afternoon.
we'll bring some beer.
it is now 2 p.m.
call meanwhile if you're interested.

   397-8211

Steve and Frank

on the sunny banks of the university

I think that all the decades of teaching English
Lit has gotten to him.

his own writing has become more and more
comfortable.
he has survived, he has held on to his job, he has
changed wives (often).
but it was all just too easy, really, teaching those Lit
classes
and coasting along and by
doing that he has missed out on something important,
reality perhaps,
and it's beginning to show.
each new book of poetry gets more and more
comfortable (as I said earlier).

I think good poetry should startle, shatter and,
yes, entertain while getting as close to the truth as
possible.
I can get all the *comfort* I need from a good
cigar.

if this gentleman expects his own poetry to be taught
by others
in future English
Lit classes
he'd better get his ass out of the warm sand
and start splashing in the bloody waters of real
life.

or maybe he'd just rather be a good old guy
forever,
adored and comforted by the eager young
coeds.
that's not so bad, really,
considering that you get paid very well for
that.

vacation in Greece

it was 4 years ago, she told me,
and we were on a private beach,
on the Mediterranean
my sister and I—
my sister is 18 and she has
long and lovely
legs,
and these 3 beautiful young men
bronzed and slim
put their blankets near ours;
one was an Englishman, one was a Scotsman
and the other might have been
Greek or Italian.
my sister and I started spreading oil on our
bodies, you
know, and it was all going well, you could
feel the vibes—
then this boy of 12 walked up,
he was bowlegged, had acne,
a very *scruffy* boy,
and he started speaking to the men
and the men talked to him
and one of the men gave him a cigarette
and the boy stood there
smoking the cigarette
not inhaling
and then one of the men got up
and went into the water with the boy
behind some rocks
where the water was shallow
and the man and the boy
stayed there quite a while.

then they came back.
then
the men got up, folded their blankets
and walked off.
the boy stood there
smoking another cigarette, not
inhaling.
I asked him:
"how did you get in here? it's a
private beach."
the boy pointed to a fence behind us.
"it was easy," he said, "there'a hole in
the fence."
his English was terrible.
and then he walked away along the shore with his bowlegs,
such a *scruffy* boy.

the spill

the jock's horse
the 7 horse
clipped the heels
of the horse
in front of
him

stumbled and
fell
throwing the
jock
over its
head
and onto the
track before
some
oncoming
horses

most of
which
avoided the
jock's
still
form

except for
the 9
horse

who gave him
one step
in the middle
of his
back

you could
see
the hoof
dig
in

then the
field was
past
and the
ambulance was
on its
way

the jock wore
Kelly green
silks,
black
sleeves.

3 or 4
people were now
gathered around
the
still
jock.

as the ambulance
moved in

the man behind
me
said to his
companion,
"let's go get
a
beer."

the last salamander

it's freezing again, and the snitch is sucking up
to the warden. I'm down $20 with six to go, someone stole
the bell and Darlene broke her left kneecap; the hunter
weeps in the bracken, and in the mirror I see pennies for
eyes; this war is like a dead green shawl
as the last salamander
gets ready to
die.
I am down $50 with four to go,
the boy broke the mower on an apricot and
the skyscraper trembles in the bleeding January night.
I am down $100 with two to go, I will double up
face down, go for broke, and it
might be time for a trip to Spain or to buy
one last pair of new shoes.
it gets sad; the walls grip my
fingers and smile;
I know who killed Cock Robin; I know who tricked Benny
the Dip; and
now somebody is picking the lock and the searchlights are
out of focus.
I'm down $500 with one to go,
my horse explodes in the middle of the dream,
it's really freezing now, can't
get it up
can't
get it down
can't
get it;
a chorus of purple songbirds
shakes the trees; I watch a parade of wooden monkeys
burn; as the tin cock crows, I just don't
understand.

learning the ropes

he was my guru.
he was a big man, bearded, self-assured.
he sat in one chair.
I sat in another.
we had been up together many days
and nights.

there had been an hour's heavy
silence.
then he leaned forward slightly
and whispered,
"you don't have to worry about
worms when you die, Chinaski,
worms don't infest dead
bodies, it's a fairy tale."

"that's good to know," I
said.

then we fell into another
hour's heavy
silence.

bombed away

when I was younger
when we were all younger
one of T. S. Eliot's most admired
and envied
lines
was:
"this is the way the world
ends,
not with a bang
but a
whimper."

before Hiroshima
we all wished we had written that immortal
line.

however
poor T.S. lost
much of his immortality
because of that
monstrous
event.

but at least
he had his immortal status
for a
while

and like the old fighter
Beau Jack said
after blowing his fortune on
parties, suckerfish and
women:

"it beats not ever having been
the champ."

these days
we don't know how
or
when
the world will
conclude.

and under the circumstances,
the idea of
an immortal line or poem
seems somewhat
optimistic

not to mention the fact that
most of us now
do our whimpering long
before any possible
end.

the swimming pool will be going here

Mr. Cobweb, call me when the applause breaks out like a sprinkle of
henshit; 1671 wasn't so long ago and tomorrow waits like a headless
anvil; but I'm still able to reach for my handkerchief
and wave to the ever-dancing girls (what dolls!) stomping away as
my brain in that dark cellar simmers in the stew.
sure, good things keep happening, eh? I mean, sometimes I fear
that I'm going to explode right through the top of my skull:
teeth, lungs, intestines, liver, bladder, balls and all, and
for hardly any *reason*! I've
got to be nuts, you
know! hope
so.

Mr. Cobweb, call me, I have an answering service, and oh yes, my friend
the great actor stuck his foot down into the dirt behind his mansion in
Malibu Canyon and told me: "the swimming pool will be going
here."

mainly, though, what I like is how the sun keeps on trying and we
build sidewalks and walk on them, we go up and down in elevators, read
newspapers, take issue with events singular and worldly, keep exercising,
we keep going and going, it's all rather fresh and exciting,
and new girls continue to get up to dance, those beautiful dancing
girls, I clutch the blade in my teeth and grin at them, Mr.
Cobweb!
and, Mr. Cobweb, there was another great actor, he was sitting with
his drink, looking down into his drink, he had a long thin sad neck
and I walked over and said, "listen, Harry, you're always depressed, get
over it, you're at the top of your game, things could be a lot worse, you
could be servicing Hondas at Jiffy Lube . . ."

Mr. Cobweb, even 1332 wasn't so long ago, we are all blessed in this life,
looking around and trying to fit ourselves into the puzzle, it takes time,
a lifetime, many lifetimes, but we have to keep trying and that takes guts.
me? shit, I've had enough, it's grand, sure, but let me nudge
out now. I distrust the whole tawdry game.

Mr. Cobweb, Al Capone has been dead a long time but it doesn't seem so
long to me, I sit within these brown-yellow walls and there's an old
rose stuck in an old drinking glass, it's been there several months looking
at me and I reach out and touch it—the petals are still there but
they feel strangely like paper; why shouldn't they, huh?

Mr. Cobweb, you tell the funniest jokes I've ever heard!

so call me any time, I always answer on the fourth ring, for
sure.

a bright boy

I was in one of those after-hour places.
I don't know how long I had been there when
I noticed a dead cigar in my hand. I attempted
to light it and burned my nose.

"you ever meet Randy Newhall?" the guy
next to me asked.

"no . . ."

"he went through college in 2 years instead
of 4."

I asked the barkeep to bring us a couple more
drinks.

"then he walked into the largest employment agency
in town, they had 50 applications for this
one job at a talent agency but
he just talked to the manager for 15
minutes and was hired."

"uh . . ."

"he began in the mailroom and in 12 months he
was making package deals for tv programs
and movies.
nobody ever got out of the mailroom that
fast, and next he married a rich girl
just out of law school."

"yeah?"

"after that he spent most of his
time putting golf balls into a water glass
in his office.
he made the work look easy . . ."

"listen," I asked, "what time is it? the
battery in my watch went dead."

". . . and in another year
he was promoted to upper management and
a year later he took over the whole place.
he was
the youngest CEO in America."

"you buy the next round," I told him.

"sure, well, he doubled his work hours and
after a while his wife left him—women don't
understand."

"what?"

"guys like him."

"oh . . ."

"he didn't contest the divorce.
he just moved on. it didn't faze him one bit.
it was amazing, you'd
see him having dinner with congressmen, with
the mayor."

"are you going to get the next round?"

he told the barkeep, who brought two more.

"then he began working 16- and 18-
hour days and after work he'd frequent
after-hour places above the Sunset Strip, to relax,
to try to unwind."

"a place like this, huh?"

"this *was* the place. he didn't try to close
deals, he just wanted to relax with the
actors, the artists, the screenwriters, the
directors, the producers, the investors
and so forth. and, of course, there were also the
beautiful girls."

"here?"

"yes, look around . . ."

I did.

"well, it was just a matter of time until he discovered
coke, then more coke, mostly with his new friends
after the after-hour places closed."

"flying, what?"

"yes, but professionally he
continued to function well until
he began doing crank."

"it really keeps you awake, huh? my
round to buy . . ."

I ordered two more.

"after some months he felt more and more
depressed, he took 6 weeks off and went to
Hawaii, resting, laying in the sun."

"did he screw?"

"he told me that he tried. anyhow, he came back
and he used to talk to me here just like you're
doing now."

"oh."

"then he became obsessed with some Mexican Real
Estate Dream
which
he would bankroll
with a Mexican friend
who was powerful in politics there.
the master plan was that
within 8 years they would control
a real estate empire and
several banks before the
government could stop them.

"drink up," I suggested.

"well, they didn't quite get it rolling.
he lost everything.
at the office he became difficult and unreasonable,
smashing ashtrays, throwing the phone out the window,
once pouring a can of Tab down his secretary's
blouse. yet somehow he managed to retain an
obnoxious brilliance and he remained almost function-
al which was better than most of the others there."

"most others don't have much."

"that's true. anyhow, one day he arrived at work
dressed in a house painter's outfit, you know, the
white overalls, the little white cap, carrying a brush and a
bucket of paint. that's when the Board of Directors
insisted on a 3-month leave of absence."

"BARKEEP!" I yelled. "COUPLE MORE!"

"he sold his house and moved into an apart-
ment on Fountain Avenue. his friends came by for
a while, then they stopped."

"suckerfish like winners."

"yes, and then there was a period when he tried to
get back with his x-wife but she didn't want any more
of that. she was with a young sculptor from Boston
who was immensely talented and who taught
at an Ivy League university."

"a rough turn of events," I said.

"anyhow, our friend had this apartment
on Fountain Avenue and
one day the manager who lived in the apartment
below noticed water coming down through the
ceiling . . ."

"oh?"

"he ran upstairs and knocked on the door, there
was no answer, he took out his key and opened it, went
in and there was Randy standing there like a statue,
his head down in the bathroom sink, the water
running and overflowing,
running over the floor, and the manager wasn't sure what
to think, it looked so strange, and he went over and
saw that the head was wedged there in the sink,
and the manager felt his legs, his back, and everything
was stiff, *rigor mortis* had long ago set in, there he
was standing with his head down under the water
and the overhead light on . . ."

"listen, Monty," I said, "your name is 'Monty,' isn't
it?"

"yes, you've got it right."

"I drove over here earlier but that was such a long time ago.
do you remember if the parking lot is out front
or in the back?"

"it's straight out back."

"goodnight, Monty."

"goodnight."

fortunately after all that
I still knew front from back. I climbed down off
that bar stool and made my way as best I could to the
exit.

my turn

the male reviewer writes that he
misses the poems about
the drinking bouts and the hard
women and the low
life.

the female reviewer says that
all I write about
is drinking and puking and bad
women
and a life nobody could
ever care
about.

their reviews are
on the same page
and are about
the same book

and
this is a poem
about
book reviewers.

skinny-dipping

as a young man
he went skinny-dipping with
Kafka
but it was too much
for him:
the sun burned him badly
and he was in bed
for two days
with a high
fever.
he was fat
and in great pain
as he twisted in the
sheets.

now Kafka didn't get burned
and he visited the fat
boy
and the fat boy's
mother
gave Kafka
hell.

and life continued.

and the fat boy
went on to write many
books and he became
famous in his own
time
while Kafka only wrote
a few books and remained
unknown.

the fat boy
even went on to live
comfortably in Paris
with a wife of some
importance
and they mixed with
many of the
great artists of their
day

while Kafka remained
unknown

and life continued.

a close call

pushing my cart through the supermarket
today
the thought crossed my mind
that I could start
knocking cans from the shelves and swiping
at rolls of towels, toilet paper and
silver foil,
I could throw oranges, bananas, tomatoes
into the air, I could take cans of
beer from the refrigerator and roll
them down the aisle, I could pull up
women's skirts and grab their asses,
I could ram my shopping cart through
the plate glass window.

then another thought occurred to me:
people generally consider the consequences
before they do something
like that.

I pushed my cart along.

a young woman in a checkered skirt was
bending over in the pet food section.
I seriously considered grabbing her
ass
but I didn't, I rolled on
by.

I had the items I needed and I pushed
my cart up to the checkout stand.
a lady in a red smock with a nameplate

waited on me.
the nameplate indicated her name was
"Robin."

Robin looked at me: "how you doing?"
she asked.

"fine," I told her.

and then she began tabulating and
bagging my purchases
with no idea that
the fellow standing there before her
had just two minutes ago been
one small step away from the
madhouse.

like a rock

through early evening
I
sit alone
listening to the sound of
the heater;
I fall into myself
like a rock dropped into some
ungrand canyon.
it hits bottom. I
lift my drink.

unfortunately
my hell is not any more hell
than the hell of a
fly.

that's what makes it
difficult. and
nothing is less
profound than a
melancholy
drunk.

I must remember:
the death or the murder of a
drunk matters
less
than
nothing.

spider, on the wall:
why do you take
so long?

the waitress at the yogurt shop

is young, quite young,
and the boys are lined up on the bench
waiting for a table
as she waits on customers.

the boys say sly and
daring things to her
in very low voices.

they all want to
bed down with her
or
at least
get her
attention.

she hears the
whispered remarks,
really likes hearing them
but says,
again and again,
"shut up! oh, you shut up!"

it goes on and
on:
the boys continue and
she continues:
"oh, shut up!"

in a voice without
grace or melody
in a voice
without warmth or humor
in a voice
remarkably
ugly:

"*oh, shut up now!*"

but the eager boys
are not aware of her
tone of
voice

and the one who will
finally live with that
voice
is probably not yet sitting
there.

her husband of the
future
will finally understand
the horrible reality of
that voice

(remember,
the voice is the window
to the soul)

and he will think:

oh my god
oh my god
oh my god

what have I
done?

won't
she
ever

shut up?

one out in the minor leagues

men on 2nd and 3rd.
first base was open.
one out.
we gave Parker an
intentional walk.
we had a 3-to-2
lead.
last half of the
9th, Simpson on the
mound.
Tanner up.
Simpson let it go.
it was low and
inside.
Tanner tapped it
to our shortstop,
DeMarco.
perfect double play
ball.
DeMarco gloved it,
flipped it to Johnson
our 2b man.
Johnson touched 2nd
then stood there
holding the ball as
the runners were
steaming around
the bases.
I screamed at Johnson
from the dugout:
"DO SOMETHING WITH THE
GODDAMNED BALL!"

the whole stadium was
screaming.
Johnson just stood there
a funny look on his face
with the ball.
then
he fell forward
still holding the ball.
he was
stretched out there as
the winning run
scored.

the dugout emptied
as we ran
to Johnson.
we turned him
over.
he wasn't moving.
he looked
dead.
the trainer took
his pulse and
looked at me.
then he started
mouth-to-mouth.

the announcer asked
if there was a
doctor in the
stands.

two of them came
down.
one of them
was drunk.

the tiny crowd started
coming
out on the field.
the ushers pushed
them back.

somebody took the
ball out of Johnson's
hand.

they worked on him
for a long time.
there was a
camera flash.
then another.
then the doctor
stood up:

"it's no good.
he's gone."

the stretcher
came out and
we loaded Johnson
onto the stretcher.

somebody threw a
warm-up
jacket
over his face.

the stadium was
almost deserted as
they carried Johnson
off the field
through
the dugout
and into
the locker room.

I didn't go
in.
I took a cup of water
from the cooler
and
sat alone on the bench.

Toby the batboy
came over.
"what's going to happen now, Mr.
Quinn?" he asked.

"our 2nd baseman is
dead, Toby."

"who you going to play
there now?"

"I don't think that's
important right now," I
told him.

"yes, it is, Mr. Quinn!
we're 2 games out of
first place
going into September!"

"I'll think of something,
Toby . . ."

then I got up and went
through the door
to the locker room,
Toby following right
behind.

the little girls hissed

since my last name was Fuch, he said to Raymond, you can
believe the school yard was tough: they put itching
powder down my neck, threw gravel at me, stung me
with rubber bands in class, and outside they called
me names, well, one name mainly, over and over,
and on top of all that my parents were poor, I wore
cardboard in my shoes to fill in the holes in the
soles, my pants were patched, my shirts thread-
bare; and even my teachers ganged up
on me, they slammed my
palm with rulers and sent me to the principal's office as
if I was really guilty of something;
and, of course, the abuse kept coming from my classmates;
I was stoned, beaten, pissed on;
the little girls hissed and stuck their tongues out
at me . . .

Fuch's wife smiled sadly at Raymond: my poor darling husband had such
a *terrible* childhood!
(she was so beautiful it almost stunned one to look at
her.)

Fuch looked at Raymond: hey, your glass is empty.

yeah, said Raymond.

Fuch touched a button and the English butler silently
glided in. he nodded respectfully to Raymond and in his
beautiful accent asked, another drink, sir?

yes, please, Raymond answered.

the butler went off to prepare the drink.

what hurt most, of course, continued Fuch, was the name-
calling.

Raymond asked, have you never forgotten it?

I did for a while, but then strangely I began to
miss the abuse . . .

the butler returned carrying Raymond's
drink on a silver tray.

here is your drink, sir, said the butler.

thank you, said Raymond, taking it off the tray.

o.k., Paul, Fuch said to the butler, you can
start now.

now? asked the butler.

now, came the answer.

the butler stood in front of Fuch and screamed:
fucky-boy! fucky-baby! fuck-face! fuck-brain!
where did your name come from, fuck-head?
how come you're such a fuck-up?
etc. . . .

they all started laughing uncontrollably
as the butler delivered his tirade in that
beautiful British accent.

they couldn't stop laughing, they fell out of their
chairs and got down on the rug, pounding it and
laughing, Fuch, his lovely young wife and Raymond
in that sprawling mansion overlooking the shining sea.

I dreamt

that I was
in my room

having been
shot in the belly
by some tart.

snakes crawled the
floor

while outside
a schoolmaster
sang
an old school
song

then

the curtains
went up in
flame

the phone
rang

everything
seemed
in a hurry
to die

so I
decided to
die

which made all the
bad poets
happy
and all the good poets
glad

as they
rushed in
to fill
the vacancy

then the dream
was
over

I awakened
and I was

the Bad Boy
of poetry

all over
again.

the old couple next door

they were an old couple
and she slept with her
head at one end of the
bed
and he with his head
at the other
end.
they explained that
in case somebody
came in to murder
them
at least one of them
would have a
better chance to
escape.

when he died
she had a stuffed replica
made of his
body
and she slept with
her head at one end
of the bed
and the replica's
head was down at the
other.

and just like in the
past,
at least once every
night,

she would awaken
in a fury and
scream,
"STOP
THAT
GODDAMNED
SNORING!"

men without women

finally,
goaded by the high price of
female relationships
he lashed his ankles to the
bedpoles
and tried to reach his
own
penis
with his
mouth:
close but no
cigar.
another of
nature's dirty
tricks.

finally, in a
fury, he gave it a last
mad
attempt.

something cracked in his
back
and a blue flame
engulfed his
brain.

after 45 minutes of
agony
he got himself off
the bed,

found he couldn't stand
straight.
each time he tried
a hundred knives cut
into both his back and
his soul.

the next day
he managed to drive to
the doctor's
office
bent low over the
steering wheel
barely able to
see through the
windshield.

"how did you do this?"
the
doctor
asked.

he told the doctor
the honest
truth
because he felt
that an informed
diagnosis
was the only chance
for a complete
cure.

"what?" said the
doctor. "you're
kidding?"

"no, that's what
happened."

"please excuse me,
I'll be right
back."

there was a dead
silence.
then he heard the
soft laughter of
the doctor and the
nurse from
behind the door.
then it grew
louder.

he sat there
looking out the office
window: there was a park outside
with lovely mature trees, it was
a fine summer afternoon
the birds were out in force and
for some odd reason
he longed for a shimmering bowl
of cool wet grapes.

the laughter behind the door
grew softer again
and then died out
as he sat there
waiting.

the "Beats"

some keep trying to connect me with
the "Beats"
but I was almost unpublished in the
1950s
and
even then
I very much
distrusted their vanity and
all that
public
posturing.

and when I met a few of them
later in life
I realized that most of my original
feelings for
them
hadn't
changed.

some of my friends accepted
that; others thought that I
should change my
opinion.

my opinion remains the
same: writing is done
one person
at a time
one place
at a time

and all the gatherings
of
the
flock
have very little
to do
with
anything.

any one of them
could have made
a decent living as a
bill collector or a
used car
salesman

and they still
could
make an honest living
instead of bitching about
changes of fashion and
the ways of fate.

but instead
from the sad university
lecterns
and in the poetry halls
these hucksters of the
despoiled word

are still clamoring for
handouts,
still talking the same
dumb
shit.

hurry slowly

when will you take to the cane,
Chinaski?
when will you walk that short-legged
dog into the last
sunset?
that wrinkled-nosed dog
snorting and sniffing
before you
as the sidewalks part
and the ocean roars in
bearing beautiful
mermaids.

straighten your back,
the sun is rushing past
you,
grin at the gods,
they only lent you the luck and the
mirage.

Chinaski?
you hear me?
the young girls of your dreams
have grown old.
Chinaski,
let it go,
the music has finished.
Chinaski?
Chinaski, don't you hear
me?

why do you keep trying?
nobody is watching.
nobody cares,
not even you.

you are alone, Chinaski,
and below the stage
the seats are
empty.
the theatre is dark.
why do you keep
acting?

what a bad
habit.

the air is so still,
the air is black and still as
you move through the last of
yourself,
give way, give way
old poet,
hanging by the last thread,
use your courage
write that last line,
get out, get out, get out,
get out, get out, get out,
it's easy,
the last classic
act.
the coast is clear,
now.

hello and goodbye

there's no hell like your own hell,
none can compare,
twisting in the sheets at night,
your ass freezing,
your mind on fire,
everything stupid, stupid,
as you are stuck in your poor body and in
your poor life
and it's all slowly dissolving, dissolving
into nothing.
like all the other bodies, like all the other
lives,
we all are being counted out,
taken down
by disease
by just being rubbed up against
the hard days, the harder years.
there's no escaping
this,
we just have to take it,
accept it—
or like most—
not think about it.
at all.

shoes off and on.
holidays come and gone.
hello,
goodbye.
dress, undress.
eat, sleep.

drive an automobile.
pay your taxes.
wash under the arms and
behind the neck
and scrub everything
else, for sure.

pick your coffin ahead
of time.
feel the smooth wood.
go for the soft, padded, expensive
interior.
the salesman will commend you
on your good
taste.

then horrify him.
tell him you want to try it for
size.

there's no hell like your own
hell and there's nobody else
ever
to share it with
you.

you might as well be the only
person left on earth.
sometimes you feel as if you
were.
and maybe you are.

meanwhile, pluck the lint from
your belly button,
accept what is,
get laid once in a while,
shake hands with nothing at all.
it's always been like this, it's always been like
this.
don't scream.
there's nobody left to hear
you.

strange things,
strange things these cities, the trees,
our feet walking the sidewalks,
the blood inside us
lubricating our
hearts,
the centuries finally shot apart
as you slip on your stockings and pull them
up over your
ankles.

I will never have

a house in the valley

with little stone men

on the lawn.

don't call me, I'll call you

once more
the typing is about
finished

poems scatter the
floor

this smoky room

the radio whispers
the symphony of a
dead
man

the lamp
looks at me
from my
left

it is late
night
moving
into
morning

I have lived
again
the lucky
hours

then the
phone
rings

son-of-a-
bitch:
impossible!

but my wife
will get
the
phone

perhaps
it's for
her

it can't be
for
me

I'd kill

anybody
who would
spoil
what

the gods
have sent
this old
fellow

once
again

as the dark
trees
shake
outside

as death
finally
is a monkey
caught
in a
cage.

taking the 8 count

"today," says the radio announcer,
"is Bastille Day.
203 years ago they stormed the Bastille,"
and that is the highlight of my day.
I have really been burnt out lately.
I go outside,
undress,
get in the pool, wrap my blue
floater around my gut
and water-jog.
I feel like an old man.
hell, I am an old man.
when I was born it was only 132 years back to
Bastille Day.
now, pains in my right leg and foot make for
a long day at the track
and the decades cling to me like
leeches,
sucking my energy and
my spirit.
but I intend to make a comeback
very soon.
I need the action, the gamble.
now I am drinking a cold beer.
I relax and just float.
suddenly things look better.
the leg and foot no longer hurt.
I even begin to feel good.
I'm not done yet!

I will remain in the arena.
hail, Bastille Day!
hail all the old dogs!
hail you!
hail me!
that last good
night is not yet here.

going going gone

my wife doesn't see much of me
anymore
since she got me this computer
for Xmas.
I never thought anything could consume
me like it
has.

the poems arrive by the
dozens
and yesterday there was even a decent bit
of prose.

I've now gone the complete route.
I once hand-printed all my poems and
stories.
then came the manual
typewriter.
then the electric typer.
and now this.

it's as if I have been reborn.
I watch the words form on the
screen
and as I watch more and more
words
form.

and, actually, the content seems
to be
as good as ever.

things get said as they have
always been said.
only now it's more like setting off
firecrackers or
exploding words into outer
space.

I've been told that the computer
can't write for me.
hell, I don't know, this thing
seems to have a
psyche
all its own
and it certainly spells
better than I
do.

there were always words
I wanted to use
but I was too lazy to
check the
spelling.
so I used a simpler version
or just didn't
bother.
now I toss the word
in,
then ask the computer if
I've got it spelled
right.

there's an old theory
that if you put ten thousand
monkeys in a room for
Eternity
they would eventually
rewrite every great novel
ever written,
word for word.

with a computer
they'd do it
in half an
hour.

anyhow, I'm more or less
one of those
monkeys now
and my wife hardly ever
sees me anymore, as I said
before.

I hear her coughing in the
next room
so I know that she is
there.

but that's enough
computer talk.

it's time for another
poem.

this is where they come for what's left of your soul

the books are selling, there are critical articles, more and
more critical articles that claim my work is, indeed,
at last, pretty damned good.
I am being taught alongside some of the masters.
a dangerous time, a most dangerous time
for me.
if I accept my new position, then I must work from that new
position.
I must then attempt to hold my ground, not
despoil it.
but I have watched too many others
soften, lose their natural force.
too much acceptance destroys.
so listen, my fine fellows and ladies, I am going to
ignore your late applause,
I intend to still play it loose, commit my errors,
enrage the entrenched and piss upon your
guardians, angels and / or devils.
I intend to do what I
have to do, what I have always done.
it's been too much fun to falter now.

you will not escape my iron grip
and I will escape
yours.

hot night

like this, sitting in my shorts, listening to a tenor
all the way from Cleveland
garnering applause on the radio.
I've never been to Cleveland.

I sit here in my shorts on a humid night
now listening to Ravel with my gut hanging out
over my shorts.
my soft white gut.
I draw on this cigar, inhale, then blow
blue smoke as
Ravel waltzes.

I read a fan letter written to me from Japan.
then I rip it once, twice, three times, trash
it.
young girls send me photos of their naked
selves.
blank-faced, I set my lighter to the photos,
turn them to twisted black
ash.

it's midnight and I'm too dumb to
sweat.

"oil and natural gas," says the man on the radio,
"we need oil and natural gas
for the nation's energy needs."

"fuck you, buddy," I say.

I scratch, yawn, rise, walk
to where my little refrigerator holds food
and drink.

it takes me 7 steps to get there.
one for each decade.

did you know that
to this very day
nobody can figure out how
they built the
pyramids?

the x-bum

it was a good training ground out there
(although there were times
of fear and madness)
and there were times when it wasn't kind
and there were times when my comrades were
cowardly
treacherous
or
debased.

it taught me also
that there was no bottom to life
you could always fall lower
into a bestial groveling
and when you reached
that point
nobody cared or would ever
care.
and then, with no feelings left, that was the strangest
feeling of them
all.

so, today I got into my BMW, drove to my
bank and picked up my American Express
Gold Card. (I always promised myself that I'd
write about that when it
happened.)

I know what people will say: "Chinaski! writing about
his American Express Gold Card! who gives a damn
about *that*? or who cares that he's now in
Who's Who in America?"

I can't think of another poet who makes people as
angry as I do.
I enjoy it
knowing that we are all brothers and sisters
in a very unkind extended
family
and I also never forget that
no matter
what the circumstances,
the park bench is never that far away
from any one of
us.

something cares

a reader writes from Germany
that a lady friend saw me interviewed
on tv and then
told him
that to kiss my face would be a
disgusting thing.

I wrote back that
she might be right, I didn't know,
I'd never actually tried
it.

but really
I don't write with my
face
I use my fingers
and this old Olympia
standard,
and with all the luck
I've had
I *should* kiss this
typer
but
I won't.

well, there, I just
did.
it was a cold kiss
but a faithful
one.

and now the machine
answers back:
I love you too,
old boy.

my cats

I know. I know.
they are limited, have different
needs and
concerns.

but I watch and learn from them.
I like the little they know,
which is so
much.

they complain but never
worry.
they walk with a surprising dignity.
they sleep with a direct simplicity that
humans just can't
understand.

their eyes are more
beautiful than our eyes.
and they can sleep 20 hours
a day
without
hesitation or
remorse.

when I am feeling
low
all I have to do is

watch my cats
and my
courage
returns.

I study these
creatures.

they are my
teachers.

6:30 a.m.

fondly embracing mad hopes in my dreams   the first intrusion
of day begins   when that young cat of mine   starts knocking
over and attacking things   at 6:30 in the
morning.   I rise to lead that   frisky rascal   down the
stairway   and open the door   where he always pauses
introspectively   until I give him a gentle boot in the ass
and then he is gone   into the blissful glory of the day   while I then
climb back up the stairway   to bed down again   with wife   who
has heard nothing   who sleeps so still   I must check
her breathing   to make certain she's alive   and finding that
she's o.k.   I pull the covers up.   I have the best hours of
sleep then   before the long drive to the racetrack
one more time   one more time   and one more time again
until I get so old   that the DMV   will take away my driver's
license   and I will have to ride the bus   out there
with the damned ghost people   son-of-a-bitch   what an
awful goddamned thought   better to stay home with wife and
cats   putter with paints   a la Henry Miller   and also
help   with the weeding   and the shopping   while the last of
the sun slants in like a golden sword.

what I need

I need a light pine kitchen, a new freezer, a picture window,
a first-alert ready-light, a pair of jogging shoes, some real
excitement, a yellow banjo, hot chips, a spark, two love birds,
sheer stockings, a touch of miracle, a March star, a true woman, a
new fantasy, a spicy sky, a charmed quark, some luck, a
VISA card, a walrus, a sunset at the beach, a well-
seasoned cigar, an antelope, a racy subject, an ideal to fight for, a
rainbow, a halcyon holiday and

a winner in the first, a winner in the second, a winner in the
third, a winner in the fourth, a winner in the
fifth.

hell, that's what I got just now: a winner in the
fifth!

couldn't you
guess?

gender benders

I'm only guessing, of course, as
usual but here goes:
when the ladies gather over
cocktails they talk about
how their husbands tend to
stifle them, smother their creative
instinct, their natural joy,
their ultimate female
selves.
without their husbands they
would float free
and thrive and grow
without limit
as they were meant to do.

but ladies, I will tell you
this:
when men gather they
never talk about their
wives.
we discuss the
Dallas Cowboys
or the new barmaid at
The Bat Cove Tavern
or about how Tyson would
kick Holyfield's ass . . .

unconcerned with
petty argument
we have floated free . . .
giant macho soaring
balloons!

WHEE!

after many nights

the last hour at the typewriter is only
good
if you've had a lucky and
productive
night,
otherwise
your time and effort have been
wasted.

this night
I feel good about the poems scattered
on the floor.

the door of this room is
open
and I can see out into the
night,
see part of the city to
my left;
see many lights—yellow, white
red, blue;
see also the moving lights
of the cars
traveling south on the
Harbor Freeway.

the lights of this city
are not at rest,
they shimmer in the
dark.

a blue tree outside the
window
looms powerful and at
peace.

my death,
after so many nights
like this,
will seem
logical,
sane
and
(like a few of my poems)
well-
written.

good morning, how are you?

$650,000 home, swimming pool, tennis court,
sauna, 4 late-model cars, a starlet wife;
he was blond, young, broad-shouldered, great
smile, great sense of humor.

he was an investor, said his starlet wife.

but he always seemed to be at home.

one afternoon
while he was playing tennis with his friends
two plainclothes cops
walked up
handcuffed him
took him
off.

it was in the papers the next day: he was a
hit man wanted for killing over fifty
men.

what bothered the neighbors most was
not who would move in next
but
when
had he found time to do it?

a reader of my work

what will you write about? he asks.
you no longer live with whores, you no
longer engage in barroom brawls, what
will you write about?

he seems to think that I've manufactured
a life to suit my typewriter
and if my life gets good
my writing will get bad.

I tell him that trouble will always
arrive, never worry about
that.

he doesn't seem to understand.
he asks,
what will your readers
think?

Norman Mailer still has
his readers,
I say.

but you're different,
he says.

not at all, I say,
we're both about
25 pounds
overweight.

he stares at me
unblinking
through dull
gray
eyes.

Sumatra Cum Laude

sitting across from my lawyer, I
decide, at this time, one needs a good
lawyer, a tax accountant, a decent
auto mechanic, a sympathetic doctor and
a faithful wife, in order to
survive.
also, one needs some talent of one's own,
very few friends, a good home security
system and the ability to sleep peacefully at
night.

you need at least this much in order to
get by and naturally you also must
hope to evade a long illness and / or
senility; finally, you can only
pray for a quick clean finish with
very little subsequent mourning by everybody
closely connected.

sitting across from my lawyer, I
have these thoughts.
we are on the 16th floor of a downtown office
building
and I like my lawyer, he has fine eyes,
great manners.
also, he has gotten my ass out of
several jams.

(meanwhile, among other things, you also need
a plumber who doesn't overbill and
an honest jockey who knows where the
finish line is.)

you need all the above (and more) before
you can go home with a clear mind, open a
wooden box labeled *Sumatra Cum
Laude*, take one out, light it
and take a quick puff or two
before the bluebird leaves
your shoulder,
before the snow melts,
and before the rain and the traffic
and our hurly-burly life
churn everything into
black
slush.

the disease of existence

dark, dark, dark.
humanity's shadow
shrouds the moon.
the process is
eternal.

once, I imagined that
in my old age
there would be
peace,
but not this:
dark humanity's
insufferable
relentless
presence.

humanity claws
at me
as persistently
now
as in the
beginning.
I was not born to be
one with them
yet here I am
with only
the thought
of death
and that final
separation
to comfort me.

so there's no chance,
no
hope,
just this waiting,
sitting here
tonight
surrounded
unsure
caught
transfixed,
the hours, the years,
this minute,
mutilated.

another comeback

climbing back up out of the ooze, out of
the thick black tar,
rising up again, a modern
Lazarus.
you're amazed at your good
fortune.
somehow you've had more
than your share of second
chances.
hell, accept it.
what you have, you have.
you walk and look in the bathroom
mirror
at an idiot's smile.
you know your luck.
some go down and never climb back up.
something is being kind to you.
you turn from the mirror and walk into the
world.
you find a chair, sit down, light a cigar.
back from a thousand wars
you look out from an open door into the silent
night.
Sibelius plays on the radio.
nothing has been lost or destroyed.
you blow smoke into the night,
tug at your right
ear.
baby, right now, you've got it
all.

two nights before my 72nd birthday

sitting here on a boiling hot night while
drinking a bottle of cabernet sauvignon
after winning $232 at the track.
there's not much I can tell you except
if it weren't for my bad right leg
I don't feel much different than I did
30 or 40 years ago (except that
now I have more money and should be able
to afford a decent
burial). also,
I drive better automobiles and have
stopped carrying a
switchblade.
I am still looking for a hero, a role model,
but can't find one.
I am no more tolerant of Humanity
than I ever was.
I am not bored with myself and find
that I am the only one I can
turn to in time of
crisis.
I've been ready to die for decades and
I've been practicing, polishing up
for that end
but it's very
hot tonight
and I can think of little but
this fine cabernet,
that's gift enough for me.
sometimes I can't
believe I've come this far,
this has to be some kind of goddamned

miracle!
just another old guy
blinking at the forces,
smiling a little,
as the cities tremble and the left
hand rises,
clutching
something
real.

have we come to this?

Lord, boys,
it's been a long time since we
sang a happy tune from
deep in the lungs.
somehow we've allowed them
to shut off our air, our water, our
electricity, our joy.

we've become like them: stilted, exact,
graven,
secretly bitter, smitten by
what's small.

Lord, boys,
we've not been kind enough to hippies and
harpies, to sots and slatterns,
to our brothers and
sisters.

Lord, boys,
where has the heroic self
gone?
it's gone into hiding, a scattered cat
in a hailstorm!

have we come to this?
have we really come to
this?

as I open my mouth
to sing
a happy tune from

deep in the lungs
a black fly
circles and swoops
in.

Lord!

old poem

what an old poem this is
from an old guy.

you've heard it many times
before:

me sitting here
sotted
again.

ashtray full.

bottles about.

poems scattered on the
floor.

as night creeps toward dawn
I make
more and more typing
errors and

the bars closed long
ago.

even the crickets are
asleep.

Li Po must have
experienced all these things
too.

hello, Li Po, you
juicehead, the world is still
full of
rancor and
regret.

you knew what to do
about that:
set fire to the
poems and then
sail them down the river
as the Emperor wept at such
waste

(but you and I
know that waste is a
natural part of the
way).

and the way is
now
and
fortunately
I have one drink
left
there on the floor
among the
poems
as

out of smokes
I poke into the
ashtray
light a butt
burn my nose
singe my
eyebrows

then tap out
another line of
boozy poesy

as I hear a voice
rising from the
neighborhood:
"FUCK YOU AND THAT
MACHINE!"

ah, they've been very
patient: it's 3:45
a.m.

I will now stop
typing and I will
savor this last
drink
because while

I have defeated death
at least
10,000 times

the L.A. police department
is another
matter.

older

I'm older but I don't mind,
yet.
I feel like a tank
rolling over and through all
the accumulated
crap.
more and more of it
piles up
as time passes,
physical and spiritual
crap.
we've even polluted
the stratosphere with
space junk,
with crap,
it floats around up
there.

I remember my grandmother.
she was *old*.
a mound of useless flesh
with dead eyes,
and a mind stuffed with,
well, crap.

it made me tired and
discouraged to look
at her.

me, I'm still rare meat,
I'll make a good meal,
the black dogs of death trail me,

nip at my heels.
tiresome hounds, they never
quit.

when they bring me down
they'll have something
worthy
of their efforts.
young maidens in far-off
countries will
weep,
and rightfully so.

and hell for me will be something interesting and
new.

closing time

around 2 a.m.
in my small room
after turning off the poem
machine
for now
I continue to light
cigarettes and listen to
Beethoven on the
radio.
I listen with a
strange and lazy
aplomb,
knowing there's still a poem
or two left to write, and
I feel damn
fine, at long
last,
as once again I
admire the verve and gamble
of this composer
now dead for over 100
years,
who's younger and wilder
than you are
than I am.

the centuries are sprinkled
with rare magic
with divine creatures
who help us get past the common
and
extraordinary ills
that beset us.

I light the next to last
cigarette
remember all the 2 a.m.'s
of my past,
put out of the bars
at closing time,
put out on the streets
(a ragged band of
solitary lonely
humans
we were)
each walking home
alone.

this is much better: living
where I now
live
and listening to
the reassurance
the kindness
of this unexpected
SYMPHONY OF TRIUMPH:
a new life.

no leaders, please

invent yourself and then reinvent yourself,
don't swim in the same slough.
invent yourself and then reinvent yourself
and
stay out of the clutches of mediocrity.

invent yourself and then reinvent yourself,
change your tone and shape so often that they can
never
categorize you.

reinvigorate yourself and
accept what is
but only on the terms that you have invented
and reinvented.

be self-taught.

and reinvent your life because you must;
it is your life and
its history
and the present
belong only to
you.

everything hurts

when you get as old as I am you can't help thinking
about death; you know it's getting closer with every tick of
your watch: an old fart like me can go in a second,
have a stroke, or cancer, or
etc.
etc.

while the young think about locating a piece of ass
the old think about . . . *death.*

still,
age makes you appreciate small things:
like, say, you look at a grapefruit like you never
quite looked at one before, or at a bridge, or at a dog or even
just at the sidewalk, you realize you've never really seen them clearly
before.

and all the other things around you suddenly seem . . . new.

the world is now a flower, though sometimes an ugly
one.

and driving the boulevards, you watch people in their
cars and you think: each of them must finally
die.

it's strange, isn't it, that each of them must finally die?

then (I often get lucky) I will forget about death. I will
forget that I am . . . old.

I will feel 45 again. (I've always felt 45, even when
I was 16.)

as somewhere somebody waters a small potted plant,
as a plane crashes with a fierce explosion into a mountain,
as deep in the sea strange creatures move,
the poet remains manacled to his helpless
self.

husk

now I watch other men fight
for money and glory
on television
while I sit on an old couch
in the night
a wife and 5 or 6 cats
nearby.

now I sit and watch other men fight
for money and glory.

hell,
I never fought for money.

maybe I should have
but I was never that good
at it—
only sometimes
brave.

is it too late for a comeback?

a comeback from where?

now I sit and watch other men fight
for money and glory.

I sit with a soda and 3 fig bars
as the world curls and goes up in
flame around
me.

my song

ample
consternation,
plentiful
pain

restless days
and
sleepless
nights

always fighting
with all your
heart and soul
so as not
to fail at
living.

who could ask
for anything
more?

cancer

half-past nowhere
alone
in the crumbling
tower of myself

stumbling in this the
darkest
hour

the last gamble has been
lost

as I
reach
for

bone
silence.

blue

blue fish, the blue night, a blue knife—
everything is blue.
and my cats are blue: blue fur, blue claws,
blue whiskers, blue eyes.

my bed lamp shines
blue.

inside, my blue heart pumps blue blood.

my fingernails, my toenails are
blue

and around my bed floats a
blue ghost.

even the taste inside my mouth is
blue.

and I am alone and dying and
blue.

twilight musings

the drifting of the mind.

the slow loss, the leaking away.

one's demise is not very interesting.

from my bed I watch 3 birds through the east window:

one coal black, one dark brown, the

other yellow.

as night falls I watch the red lights on the bridge blink on and off.

I am stretched out in bed with the covers up to my chin.

I have no idea who won at the racetrack today.

I must go back into the hospital tomorrow.

why me?

why not?

mind and heart

unaccountably we are alone
forever alone
and it was meant to be
that way,
it was never meant
to be any other way—
and when the death struggle
begins
the last thing I wish to see
is
a ring of human faces
hovering over me—
better just my old friends,
the walls of my self,
let only them be there.

I have been alone but seldom
lonely.
I have satisfied my thirst
at the well
of my self
and that wine was good,
the best I ever had,
and tonight
sitting
staring into the dark
I now finally understand
the dark and the
light and everything
in between.

peace of mind and heart
arrives
when we accept what
is:
having been
born into this
strange life
we must accept
the wasted gamble of our
days
and take some satisfaction in
the pleasure of
leaving it all
behind.

cry not for me.

grieve not for me.

read
what I've written
then
forget it
all.

drink from the well
of your self
and begin
again.

CHARLES BUKOWSKI is one of America's best-known contemporary writers of poetry and prose, and, many would claim, its most influential and imitated poet. He was born in Andernach, Germany, to an American soldier father and a German mother in 1920, and brought to the United States at the age of three. He was raised in Los Angeles and lived there for fifty years. He published his first story in 1944 when he was twenty-four and began writing poetry at the age of thirty-five. He died in San Pedro, California, on March 9, 1994, at the age of seventy-three, shortly after completing his last novel, *Pulp* (1994).

During his lifetime he published more than forty-five books of poetry and prose, including the novels *Post Office* (1971), *Factotum* (1975), *Women* (1978), *Ham on Rye* (1982), and *Hollywood* (1989). Among his most recent books are the posthumous editions of *What Matters Most Is How Well You Walk Through the Fire: New Poems* (1999), *Open All Night: New Poems* (2000), *Beerspit Night and Cursing: The Correspondence of Charles Bukowski and Sheri Martinelli, 1960–1967* (2001), *Night Torn Mad with Footsteps: New Poems* (2001), *sifting through the madness for the word, the line, the way: new poems* (2003), *The Flash of Lightning Behind the Mountain* (2004), and *Slouching Toward Nirvana* (2005).

All of his books have now been published in translation in over a dozen languages and his worldwide popularity remains undiminished.

endless love

I've seen old married couples
sitting in their rockers
across from one another
being congratulated
for staying together 60 or 70
years,
either of whom
would
long ago have
settled for something
else, anything else,
but fate
fear and
circumstances have
bound them
eternally together;
and as we tell them
how wonderful
their great and enduring love
is
only they
really know
the truth
but they don't tell us
that from the first day they
met
somehow
it didn't mean
all that much: